Love and
Other Stories

Love and Other Stories

Anton Chekhov

MINT EDITIONS

Love and Other Stories was first published in 1895.

This edition published by Mint Editions 2021.

ISBN 9781513264776 | E-ISBN 9781513265452

Published by Mint Editions®

 MINT
EDITIONS

minteditionbooks.com

Publishing Director: Jennifer Newens
Design & Production: Rachel Lopez Metzger
Project Manager: Micaela Clark
Translated By: Constance Garnett
Typesetting: Westchester Publishing Services

Contents

LOVE

Three o'clock in the morning. The soft April night is looking in at my windows and caressingly winking at me with its stars. I can't sleep, I am so happy!

"My whole being from head to heels is bursting with a strange, incomprehensible feeling. I can't analyse it just now—I haven't the time, I'm too lazy, and there—hang analysis! Why, is a man likely to interpret his sensations when he is flying head foremost from a belfry, or has just learned that he has won two hundred thousand? Is he in a state to do it?"

This was more or less how I began my love-letter to Sasha, a girl of nineteen with whom I had fallen in love. I began it five times, and as often tore up the sheets, scratched out whole pages, and copied it all over again. I spent as long over the letter as if it had been a novel I had to write to order. And it was not because I tried to make it longer, more elaborate, and more fervent, but because I wanted endlessly to prolong the process of this writing, when one sits in the stillness of one's study and communes with one's own day-dreams while the spring night looks in at one's window. Between the lines I saw a beloved image, and it seemed to me that there were, sitting at the same table writing with me, spirits as naïvely happy, as foolish, and as blissfully smiling as I. I wrote continually, looking at my hand, which still ached deliciously where hers had lately pressed it, and if I turned my eyes away I had a vision of the green trellis of the little gate. Through that trellis Sasha gazed at me after I had said goodbye to her. When I was saying good-bye to Sasha I was thinking of nothing and was simply admiring her figure as every decent man admires a pretty woman; when I saw through the trellis two big eyes, I suddenly, as though by inspiration, knew that I was in love, that it was all settled between us, and fully decided already, that I had nothing left to do but to carry out certain formalities.

It is a great delight also to seal up a love-letter, and, slowly putting on one's hat and coat, to go softly out of the house and to carry the treasure to the post. There are no stars in the sky now: in their place there is a long whitish streak in the east, broken here and there by clouds above the roofs of the dingy houses; from that streak the whole sky is flooded with pale light. The town is asleep, but already the water-carts have come out, and somewhere in a far-away factory a whistle sounds to wake up the workpeople. Beside the postbox, slightly moist with dew, you are sure to see the clumsy figure of a house porter, wearing a bell-shaped sheepskin and carrying a stick. He is in a condition akin to catalepsy: he is not asleep or awake, but something between.

If the boxes knew how often people resort to them for the decision of their fate, they would not have such a humble air. I, anyway, almost kissed my postbox, and as I gazed at it I reflected that the post is the greatest of blessings.

I beg anyone who has ever been in love to remember how one usually hurries home after dropping the letter in the box, rapidly gets into bed and pulls up the quilt in the full conviction that as soon as one wakes up in the morning one will be overwhelmed with memories of the previous day and look with rapture at the window, where the daylight will be eagerly making its way through the folds of the curtain.

Well, to facts. . . Next morning at midday, Sasha's maid brought me the following answer: "I am delited be sure to come to us to day please I shall expect you. Your S."

Not a single comma. This lack of punctuation, and the misspelling of the word "delighted," the whole letter, and even the long, narrow envelope in which it was put filled my heart with tenderness. In the sprawling but diffident handwriting I recognised Sasha's walk, her way of raising her eyebrows when she laughed, the movement of her lips. . . But the contents of the letter did not satisfy me. In the first place, poetical letters are not answered in that way, and in the second, why should I go to Sasha's house to wait till it should occur to her stout mamma, her brothers, and poor relations to leave us alone together? It would never enter their heads, and nothing is more hateful than to have to restrain one's raptures simply because of the intrusion of some animate trumpery in the shape of a half-deaf old woman or little girl pestering one with questions. I sent an answer by the maid asking Sasha to select some park or boulevard for a rendezvous. My suggestion was readily accepted. I had struck the right chord, as the saying is.

Between four and five o'clock in the afternoon I made my way to the furthest and most overgrown part of the park. There was not a soul in the park, and the tryst might have taken place somewhere nearer in one of the avenues or arbours, but women don't like doing it by halves in romantic affairs; in for a penny, in for a pound—if you are in for a tryst, let it be in the furthest and most impenetrable thicket, where one runs the risk of stumbling upon some rough or drunken man. When I went up to Sasha she was standing with her back to me, and in that back

I could read a devilish lot of mystery. It seemed as though that back and the nape of her neck, and the black spots on her dress were saying: Hush! . . . The girl was wearing a simple cotton dress over which she had thrown a light cape. To add to the air of mysterious secrecy, her face was covered with a white veil. Not to spoil the effect, I had to approach on tiptoe and speak in a half whisper.

From what I remember now, I was not so much the essential point of the rendezvous as a detail of it. Sasha was not so much absorbed in the interview itself as in its romantic mysteriousness, my kisses, the silence of the gloomy trees, my vows. . . There was not a minute in which she forgot herself, was overcome, or let the mysterious expression drop from her face, and really if there had been any Ivan Sidoritch or Sidor Ivanitch in my place she would have felt just as happy. How is one to make out in such circumstances whether one is loved or not? Whether the love is "the real thing" or not?

From the park I took Sasha home with me. The presence of the beloved woman in one's bachelor quarters affects one like wine and music. Usually one begins to speak of the future, and the confidence and self-reliance with which one does so is beyond bounds. You make plans and projects, talk fervently of the rank of general though you have not yet reached the rank of a lieutenant, and altogether you fire off such high-flown nonsense that your listener must have a great deal of love and ignorance of life to assent to it. Fortunately for men, women in love are always blinded by their feelings and never know anything of life. Far from not assenting, they actually turn pale with holy awe, are full of reverence and hang greedily on the maniac's words. Sasha listened to me with attention, but I soon detected an absent-minded expression on her face, she did not understand me. The future of which I talked interested her only in its external aspect and I was wasting time in displaying my plans and projects before her. She was keenly interested in knowing which would be her room, what paper she would have in the room, why I had an upright piano instead of a grand piano, and so on. She examined carefully all the little things on my table, looked at the photographs, sniffed at the bottles, peeled the old stamps off the envelopes, saying she wanted them for something.

"Please collect old stamps for me!" she said, making a grave face. "Please do."

Then she found a nut in the window, noisily cracked it and ate it.

"Why don't you stick little labels on the backs of your books?" she asked, taking a look at the bookcase.

"What for?"

"Oh, so that each book should have its number. And where am I to put my books? I've got books too, you know."

"What books have you got?" I asked.

Sasha raised her eyebrows, thought a moment and said:

"All sorts."

And if it had entered my head to ask her what thoughts, what convictions, what aims she had, she would no doubt have raised her eyebrows, thought a minute, and have said in the same way: "All sorts."

Later I saw Sasha home and left her house regularly, officially engaged, and was so reckoned till our wedding. If the reader will allow me to judge merely from my personal experience, I maintain that to be engaged is very dreary, far more so than to be a husband or nothing at all. An engaged man is neither one thing nor the other, he has left one side of the river and not reached the other, he is not married and yet he can't be said to be a bachelor, but is in something not unlike the condition of the porter whom I have mentioned above.

Every day as soon as I had a free moment I hastened to my fiancée. As I went I usually bore within me a multitude of hopes, desires, intentions, suggestions, phrases. I always fancied that as soon as the maid opened the door I should, from feeling oppressed and stifled, plunge at once up to my neck into a sea of refreshing happiness. But it always turned out otherwise in fact. Every time I went to see my fiancée I found all her family and other members of the household busy over the silly trousseau. (And by the way, they were hard at work sewing for two months and then they had less than a hundred roubles' worth of things). There was a smell of irons, candle grease and fumes. Bugles scrunched under one's feet. The two most important rooms were piled up with billows of linen, calico, and muslin and from among the billows peeped out Sasha's little head with a thread between her teeth. All the sewing party welcomed me with cries of delight but at once led me off into the dining-room where I could not hinder them nor see what only husbands are permitted to behold. In spite of my feelings, I had to sit in the dining-room and converse with Pimenovna, one of the poor relations. Sasha, looking worried and excited, kept running by me with a thimble, a skein of wool or some other boring object.

"Wait, wait, I shan't be a minute," she would say when I raised imploring eyes to her. "Only fancy that wretch Stepanida has spoilt the bodice of the barège dress!"

And after waiting in vain for this grace, I lost my temper, went out of the house and walked about the streets in the company of the new cane I had bought. Or I would want to go for a walk or a drive with my fiancée, would go round and find her already standing in the hall with her mother, dressed to go out and playing with her parasol.

"Oh, we are going to the Arcade," she would say. "We have got to buy some more cashmere and change the hat."

My outing is knocked on the head. I join the ladies and go with them to the Arcade. It is revoltingly dull to listen to women shopping, haggling and trying to outdo the sharp shopman. I felt ashamed when Sasha, after turning over masses of material and knocking down the prices to a minimum, walked out of the shop without buying anything, or else told the shopman to cut her some half rouble's worth.

When they came out of the shop, Sasha and her mamma with scared and worried faces would discuss at length having made a mistake, having bought the wrong thing, the flowers in the chintz being too dark, and so on.

Yes, it is a bore to be engaged! I'm glad it's over.

Now I am married. It is evening. I am sitting in my study reading. Behind me on the sofa Sasha is sitting munching something noisily. I want a glass of beer.

"Sasha, look for the corkscrew. . ." I say. "It's lying about somewhere."

Sasha leaps up, rummages in a disorderly way among two or three heaps of papers, drops the matches, and without finding the corkscrew, sits down in silence. . . Five minutes pass—ten. . . I begin to be fretted both by thirst and vexation.

"Sasha, do look for the corkscrew," I say.

Sasha leaps up again and rummages among the papers near me. Her munching and rustling of the papers affects me like the sound of sharpening knives against each other. . . I get up and begin looking for the corkscrew myself. At last it is found and the beer is uncorked. Sasha remains by the table and begins telling me something at great length.

"You'd better read something, Sasha," I say.

She takes up a book, sits down facing me and begins moving her lips. . . I look at her little forehead, moving lips, and sink into thought.

"She is getting on for twenty. . ." I reflect. "If one takes a boy of the educated class and of that age and compares them, what a difference! The boy would have knowledge and convictions and some intelligence."

But I forgive that difference just as the low forehead and moving lips are forgiven. I remember in my old Lovelace days I have cast off women for a stain on their stockings, or for one foolish word, or for not cleaning their teeth, and now I forgive everything: the munching, the muddling about after the corkscrew, the slovenliness, the long talking about nothing that matters; I forgive it all almost unconsciously, with no effort of will, as though Sasha's mistakes were my mistakes, and many things which would have made me wince in old days move me to tenderness and even rapture. The explanation of this forgiveness of everything lies in my love for Sasha, but what is the explanation of the love itself, I really don't know.

Lights

The dog was barking excitedly outside. And Ananyev the engineer, his assistant called Von Schtenberg, and I went out of the hut to see at whom it was barking. I was the visitor, and might have remained indoors, but I must confess my head was a little dizzy from the wine I had drunk, and I was glad to get a breath of fresh air.

"There is nobody here," said Ananyev when we went out. "Why are you telling stories, Azorka? You fool!"

There was not a soul in sight.

"The fool," Azorka, a black house-dog, probably conscious of his guilt in barking for nothing and anxious to propitiate us, approached us, diffidently wagging his tail. The engineer bent down and touched him between his ears.

"Why are you barking for nothing, creature?" he said in the tone in which good-natured people talk to children and dogs. "Have you had a bad dream or what? Here, doctor, let me commend to your attention," he said, turning to me, "a wonderfully nervous subject! Would you believe it, he can't endure solitude—he is always having terrible dreams and suffering from nightmares; and when you shout at him he has something like an attack of hysterics."

"Yes, a dog of refined feelings," the student chimed in.

Azorka must have understood that the conversation was concerning him. He turned his head upwards and grinned plaintively, as though to say, "Yes, at times I suffer unbearably, but please excuse it!"

It was an August night, there were stars, but it was dark. Owing to the fact that I had never in my life been in such exceptional surroundings, as I had chanced to come into now, the starry night seemed to me gloomy, inhospitable, and darker than it was in reality. I was on a railway line which was still in process of construction. The high, half-finished embankment, the mounds of sand, clay, and rubble, the holes, the wheel-barrows standing here and there, the flat tops of the mud huts in which the workmen lived—all this muddle, coloured to one tint by the darkness, gave the earth a strange, wild aspect that suggested the times of chaos. There was so little order in all that lay before me that it was somehow strange in the midst of the hideously excavated, grotesque-looking earth to see the silhouettes of human beings and the slender telegraph posts. Both spoiled the ensemble of the picture, and seemed to belong to a different world. It was still, and the only sound came from the telegraph wire droning its wearisome refrain somewhere very high above our heads.

We climbed up on the embankment and from its height looked down upon the earth. A hundred yards away where the pits, holes, and mounds melted into the darkness of the night, a dim light was twinkling. Beyond it gleamed another light, beyond that a third, then a hundred paces away two red eyes glowed side by side—probably the windows of some hut—and a long series of such lights, growing continually closer and dimmer, stretched along the line to the very horizon, then turned in a semicircle to the left and disappeared in the darkness of the distance. The lights were motionless. There seemed to be something in common between them and the stillness of the night and the disconsolate song of the telegraph wire. It seemed as though some weighty secret were buried under the embankment and only the lights, the night, and the wires knew of it.

"How glorious, O Lord!" sighed Ananyev; "such space and beauty that one can't tear oneself away! And what an embankment! It's not an embankment, my dear fellow, but a regular Mont Blanc. It's costing millions. . ."

Going into ecstasies over the lights and the embankment that was costing millions, intoxicated by the wine and his sentimental mood, the engineer slapped Von Schtenberg on the shoulder and went on in a jocose tone:

"Well, Mihail Mihailitch, lost in reveries? No doubt it is pleasant to look at the work of one's own hands, eh? Last year this very spot was bare steppe, not a sight of human life, and now look: life. . . civilisation. . . And how splendid it all is, upon my soul! You and I are building a railway, and after we are gone, in another century or two, good men will build a factory, a school, a hospital, and things will begin to move! Eh!"

The student stood motionless with his hands thrust in his pockets, and did not take his eyes off the lights. He was not listening to the engineer, but was thinking, and was apparently in the mood in which one does not want to speak or to listen. After a prolonged silence he turned to me and said quietly:

"Do you know what those endless lights are like? They make me think of something long dead, that lived thousands of years ago, something like the camps of the Amalekites or the Philistines. It is as though some people of the Old Testament had pitched their camp and were

ANTON CHEKHOV

waiting for morning to fight with Saul or David. All that is wanting to complete the illusion is the blare of trumpets and sentries calling to one another in some Ethiopian language."

And, as though of design, the wind fluttered over the line and brought a sound like the clank of weapons. A silence followed. I don't know what the engineer and the student were thinking of, but it seemed to me already that I actually saw before me something long dead and even heard the sentry talking in an unknown tongue. My imagination hastened to picture the tents, the strange people, their clothes, their armour.

"Yes," muttered the student pensively, "once Philistines and Amalekites were living in this world, making wars, playing their part, and now no trace of them remains. So it will be with us. Now we are making a railway, are standing here philosophising, but two thousand years will pass—and of this embankment and of all those men, asleep after their hard work, not one grain of dust will remain. In reality, it's awful!"

"You must drop those thoughts. . ." said the engineer gravely and admonishingly.

"Why?"

"Because. . . Thoughts like that are for the end of life, not for the beginning of it. You are too young for them."

"Why so?" repeated the student.

"All these thoughts of the transitoriness, the insignificance and the aimlessness of life, of the inevitability of death, of the shadows of the grave, and so on, all such lofty thoughts, I tell you, my dear fellow, are good and natural in old age when they come as the product of years of inner travail, and are won by suffering and really are intellectual riches; for a youthful brain on the threshold of real life they are simply a calamity! A calamity!" Ananyev repeated with a wave of his hand. "To my mind it is better at your age to have no head on your shoulders at all than to think on these lines. I am speaking seriously, Baron. And I have been meaning to speak to you about it for a long time, for I noticed from the very first day of our acquaintance your partiality for these damnable ideas!"

"Good gracious, why are they damnable?" the student asked with a smile, and from his voice and his face I could see that he asked the question from simple politeness, and that the discussion raised by the engineer did not interest him in the least.

I could hardly keep my eyes open. I was dreaming that immediately after our walk we should wish each other good-night and go to bed, but my dream was not quickly realised. When we had returned to the hut the engineer put away the empty bottles and took out of a large wicker hamper two full ones, and uncorking them, sat down to his work-table with the evident intention of going on drinking, talking, and working. Sipping a little from his glass, he made pencil notes on some plans and went on pointing out to the student that the latter's way of thinking was not what it should be. The student sat beside him checking accounts and saying nothing. He, like me, had no inclination to speak or to listen. That I might not interfere with their work, I sat away from the table on the engineer's crooked-legged travelling bedstead, feeling bored and expecting every moment that they would suggest I should go to bed. It was going on for one o'clock.

Having nothing to do, I watched my new acquaintances. I had never seen Ananyev or the student before. I had only made their acquaintance on the night I have described. Late in the evening I was returning on horseback from a fair to the house of a landowner with whom I was staying, had got on the wrong road in the dark and lost my way. Going round and round by the railway line and seeing how dark the night was becoming, I thought of the "barefoot railway roughs," who lie in wait for travellers on foot and on horseback, was frightened, and knocked at the first hut I came to. There I was cordially received by Ananyev and the student. As is usually the case with strangers casually brought together, we quickly became acquainted, grew friendly and at first over the tea and afterward over the wine, began to feel as though we had known each other for years. At the end of an hour or so, I knew who they were and how fate had brought them from town to the far-away steppe; and they knew who I was, what my occupation and my way of thinking.

Nikolay Anastasyevitch Ananyev, the engineer, was a broad-shouldered, thick-set man, and, judging from his appearance, he had, like Othello, begun the "descent into the vale of years," and was growing rather too stout. He was just at that stage which old match-making women mean when they speak of "a man in the prime of his age," that is, he was neither young nor old, was fond of good fare, good liquor, and praising the past, panted a little as he walked, snored loudly when he was asleep, and in his manner with those surrounding him displayed that calm imperturbable good humour which is always acquired by decent people by the time they have reached the grade of a staff officer and begun to grow stout. His hair and beard were far from being grey, but already, with a condescension of which he was unconscious, he addressed young men as "my dear boy" and felt himself entitled to lecture them good-humouredly about their way of thinking. His movements and his voice were calm, smooth, and self-confident, as they are in a man who is thoroughly well aware that he has got his feet firmly planted on the right road, that he has definite work, a secure living, a settled outlook. . . His sunburnt, thicknosed face and muscular neck seemed to say: "I am well fed, healthy, satisfied with myself, and the time will come when you young people too, will be well-fed, healthy, and satisfied with yourselves. . ." He was dressed in a cotton shirt with the collar awry and in full linen trousers thrust into his high boots. From certain trifles, as for instance, from his coloured worsted girdle, his embroidered collar, and the patch on his elbow, I was able to guess that he was married and in all probability tenderly loved by his wife.

Baron Von Schtenberg, a student of the Institute of Transport, was a young man of about three or four and twenty. Only his fair hair and scanty beard, and, perhaps, a certain coarseness and frigidity in his features showed traces of his descent from Barons of the Baltic provinces; everything else—his name, Mihail Mihailovitch, his religion, his ideas, his manners, and the expression of his face were purely Russian. Wearing, like Ananyev, a cotton shirt and high boots, with his round shoulders, his hair left uncut, and his sunburnt face, he did not look like a student or a Baron, but like an ordinary Russian workman. His words and gestures were few, he drank reluctantly without relish, checked the accounts mechanically, and seemed all the while to be thinking of something else. His movements and voice were calm, and smooth too, but his calmness was of a different kind from the engineer's. His sunburnt, slightly ironical, dreamy face, his eyes which looked up from under his brows, and his whole figure were expressive of spiritual stagnatio—mental sloth. He looked as though it did not matter to him in the least whether the light were burning before him or not, whether the wine were nice or nasty, and whether the accounts he was checking were correct or not. . . And on his intelligent, calm face I read: "I don't see so far any good in definite work, a secure living, and a settled outlook. It's all nonsense. I was in Petersburg, now I am sitting here in this hut, in the autumn I shall go back to Petersburg, then in the spring here again. . . What sense there is in all that I don't know, and no one knows. . . And so it's no use talking about it. . ."

He listened to the engineer without interest, with the condescending indifference with which cadets in the senior classes listen to an effusive and good-natured old attendant. It seemed as though there were nothing new to him in what the engineer said, and that if he had not himself been too lazy to talk, he would have said something newer and cleverer. Meanwhile Ananyev would not desist. He had by now laid aside his good-humoured, jocose tone and spoke seriously, even with a fervour which was quite out of keeping with his expression of calmness. Apparently he had no distaste for abstract subjects, was fond of them, indeed, but had neither skill nor practice in the handling of them. And this lack of practice was so pronounced in his talk that I did not always grasp his meaning at once.

"I hate those ideas with all my heart!" he said, "I was infected by them myself in my youth, I have not quite got rid of them even now, and I tell you—perhaps because I am stupid and such thoughts were not the right food for my mind—they did me nothing but harm. That's easy to understand! Thoughts of the aimlessness of life, of the insignificance and transitoriness of the visible world, Solomon's 'vanity of vanities' have been, and are to this day, the highest and final stage in the realm of thought. The thinker reaches that stage and—comes to a halt! There is nowhere further to go. The activity of the normal brain is completed with this, and that is natural and in the order of things. Our misfortune is that we begin thinking at that end. What normal people end with we begin with. From the first start, as soon as the brain begins working independently, we mount to the very topmost, final step and refuse to know anything about the steps below."

"What harm is there in that?" said the student.

"But you must understand that it's abnormal," shouted Ananyev, looking at him almost wrathfully. "If we find means of mounting to the topmost step without the help of the lower ones, then the whole long ladder, that is the whole of life, with its colours, sounds, and thoughts, loses all meaning for us. That at your age such reflections are harmful and absurd, you can see from every step of your rational independent life. Let us suppose you sit down this minute to read Darwin or Shakespeare, you have scarcely read a page before the poison shows itself; and your long life, and Shakespeare, and Darwin, seem to you nonsense, absurdity, because you know you will die, that Shakespeare and Darwin have died too, that their thoughts have not saved them, nor the earth, nor you, and that if life is deprived of meaning in that way, all science, poetry, and exalted thoughts seem only useless diversions, the idle playthings of grown up people; and you leave off reading at the second page. Now, let us suppose that people come to you as an intelligent man and ask your opinion about war, for instance: whether it is desirable, whether it is morally justifiable or not. In answer to that terrible question you merely shrug your shoulders and confine yourself to some commonplace, because for you, with your way of thinking, it makes absolutely no difference whether hundreds of thousands of people die a violent death, or a natural one: the results are the same—ashes and oblivion. You and I are building a railway line. What's the use, one may ask, of our worrying our heads, inventing, rising above the hackneyed thing, feeling for the workmen, stealing or not stealing, when we know that this railway line will turn to dust within two thousand years, and so on, and so on. . . You must admit that with such a disastrous way of looking at things there can be no progress, no science, no art, nor even thought itself. We fancy that we are cleverer than the crowd, and than Shakespeare. In reality our thinking leads to nothing because we have no inclination to go down to the lower steps and there is nowhere higher to go, so our brain stands at the freezing point—neither up nor down; I was in bondage to these ideas for six years, and by all that is holy, I never read a sensible book all that time, did not gain a ha'porth of wisdom, and did not raise my moral standard an inch. Was not that disastrous? Moreover, besides being corrupted ourselves, we bring poison into the lives of those surrounding us. It would be all right if, with our pessimism, we renounced life, went to live in a cave, or made haste to die, but, as it is, in obedience to the universal law, we live, feel, love women, bring up children, construct railways!"

"Our thoughts make no one hot or cold," the student said reluctantly.

"Ah! there you are again!—do stop it! You have not yet had a good sniff at life. But when you have lived as long as I have you will know a thing or two! Our theory of life is not so innocent as you suppose. In practical life, in contact with human beings, it leads to nothing but horrors and follies. It has been my lot to pass through experiences which I would not wish a wicked Tatar to endure."

"For instance?" I asked.

"For instance?" repeated the engineer.

He thought a minute, smiled and said:

"For instance, take this example. More correctly, it is not an example, but a regular drama, with a plot and a dénouement. An excellent lesson! Ah, what a lesson!"

He poured out wine for himself and us, emptied his glass, stroked his broad chest with his open hands, and went on, addressing himself more to me than to the student.

"It was in the year 187—, soon after the war, and when I had just left the University. I was going to the Caucasus, and on the way stopped for five days in the seaside town of N. I must tell you that I was born and grew up in that town, and so there is nothing odd in my thinking N. extraordinarily snug, cosy, and beautiful, though for a man from Petersburg or Moscow, life in it would be as dreary and comfortless as in any Tchuhloma or Kashira. With melancholy I passed by the high school where I had been a pupil; with melancholy I walked about the very familiar park, I made a melancholy attempt to get a nearer look at people I had not seen for a long time—all with the same melancholy.

"Among other things, I drove out one evening to the so-called Quarantine. It was a small mangy copse in which, at some forgotten time of plague, there really had been a quarantine station, and which was now the resort of summer visitors. It was a drive of three miles from the town along a good soft road. As one drove along one saw on the left the blue sea, on the right the unending gloomy steppe; there was plenty of air to breathe, and wide views for the eyes to rest on. The copse itself lay on the seashore. Dismissing my cabman, I went in at the familiar gates and first turned along an avenue leading to a little stone summer-house which I had been fond of in my childhood. In my opinion that round, heavy summer-house on its clumsy columns, which combined the romantic charm of an old tomb with the ungainliness of a Sobakevitch,* was the most poetical nook in the whole town. It stood at the edge above the cliff, and from it there was a splendid view of the sea.

"I sat down on the seat, and, bending over the parapet, looked down. A path ran from the summer-house along the steep, almost overhanging cliff, between the lumps of clay and tussocks of burdock. Where it ended, far below on the sandy shore, low waves were languidly foaming and softly purring. The sea was as majestic, as infinite, and as forbidding as seven years before when I left the high school and went from my native town to the capital; in the distance there was a dark streak of smoke—a steamer was passing—and except for this hardly visible and motionless streak and the sea-swallows that flitted over the water, there

---

* A character in Gogol's *Dead Souls.—Translator's Note.*

ANTON CHEKHOV

was nothing to give life to the monotonous view of sea and sky. To right and left of the summer-house stretched uneven clay cliffs.

"You know that when a man in a melancholy mood is left *tête-à-tête* with the sea, or any landscape which seems to him grandiose, there is always, for some reason, mixed with melancholy, a conviction that he will live and die in obscurity, and he reflectively snatches up a pencil and hastens to write his name on the first thing that comes handy. And that, I suppose, is why all convenient solitary nooks like my summer-house are always scrawled over in pencil or carved with penknives. I remember as though it were to-day; looking at the parapet I read: 'Ivan Korolkov, May 16, 1876.' Beside Korolkov some local dreamer had scribbled freely, adding:

> "*He stood on the desolate ocean's strand,*
> *While his soul was filled with imaginings grand.'*

And his handwriting was dreamy, limp like wet silk. An individual called Kross, probably an insignificant, little man, felt his unimportance so deeply that he gave full licence to his penknife and carved his name in deep letters an inch high. I took a pencil out of my pocket mechanically, and I too scribbled on one of the columns. All that is irrelevant, however. . . You must forgive me—I don't know how to tell a story briefly.

"I was sad and a little bored. Boredom, the stillness, and the purring of the sea gradually brought me to the line of thought we have been discussing. At that period, towards the end of the 'seventies, it had begun to be fashionable with the public, and later, at the beginning of the 'eighties, it gradually passed from the general public into literature, science, and politics. I was no more than twenty-six at the time, but I knew perfectly well that life was aimless and had no meaning, that everything was a deception and an illusion, that in its essential nature and results a life of penal servitude in Sahalin was not in any way different from a life spent in Nice, that the difference between the brain of a Kant and the brain of a fly was of no real significance, that no one in this world is righteous or guilty, that everything was stuff and nonsense and damn it all! I lived as though I were doing a favour to some unseen power which compelled me to live, and to which I seemed to say: 'Look, I don't care a straw for life, but I am living!' I thought on one definite line, but in all sorts of keys, and in that respect I was like the subtle gourmand who could prepare a hundred appetising dishes from nothing but potatoes. There is no doubt that I was one-sided and even to some extent narrow, but I fancied at the time that my intellectual horizon had neither beginning nor end, and that my thought was as boundless as the sea. Well, as far as I can judge by myself, the philosophy of which we are speaking has something alluring, narcotic in its nature, like tobacco or morphia. It becomes a habit, a craving. You take advantage of every minute of solitude to gloat over thoughts of the aimlessness of life and the darkness of the grave. While I was sitting in the summer-house, Greek children with long noses were decorously walking about the avenues. I took advantage of the occasion and, looking at them, began reflecting in this style:

"'Why are these children born, and what are they living for? Is there any sort of meaning in their existence? They grow up, without themselves knowing what for; they will live in this God-forsaken, comfortless hole for no sort of reason, and then they will die. . .'

"And I actually felt vexed with those children because they were walking about decorously and talking with dignity, as though they did not hold their little colourless lives so cheap and knew what they were living for. . . I remember that far away at the end of an avenue three feminine figures came into sight. Three young ladies, one in a pink dress, two in white, were walking arm-in-arm, talking and laughing. Looking after them, I thought:

"'It wouldn't be bad to have an affair with some woman for a couple of days in this dull place.'

"I recalled by the way that it was three weeks since I had visited my Petersburg lady, and thought that a passing love affair would come in very appropriately for me just now. The young lady in white in the middle was rather younger and better looking than her companions, and judging by her manners and her laugh, she was a high-school girl in an upper form. I looked, not without impure thoughts, at her bust, and at the same time reflected about her: 'She will be trained in music and manners, she will be married to some Greek—God help us!—will lead a grey, stupid, comfortless life, will bring into the world a crowd of children without knowing why, and then will die. An absurd life!'

"I must say that as a rule I was a great hand at combining my lofty ideas with the lowest prose.

"Thoughts of the darkness of the grave did not prevent me from giving busts and legs their full due. Our dear Baron's exalted ideas do not prevent him from going on Saturdays to Vukolovka on amatory expeditions. To tell the honest truth, as far as I remember, my attitude to women was most insulting. Now, when I think of that high-school girl, I blush for my thoughts then, but at the time my conscience was perfectly untroubled. I, the son of honourable parents, a Christian, who had received a superior education, not naturally wicked or stupid, felt not the slightest uneasiness when I paid women *Blutgeld*, as the Germans call it, or when I followed high-school girls with insulting looks. . . The trouble is that youth makes its demands, and our philosophy has nothing in principle against those demands, whether they are good or whether they are loathsome. One who knows that life is aimless and death inevitable is not interested in the struggle against nature or the conception of sin: whether you struggle or whether you don't, you will die and rot just the same. . . Secondly, my friends, our philosophy instils even into very young people what is called reasonableness. The predominance of reason over the heart is simply overwhelming amongst us. Direct feeling, inspiration—everything is choked by petty analysis. Where there is reasonableness there is coldness, and cold people—it's no use to disguise it—know nothing of chastity. That virtue is only known to those who are warm, affectionate, and capable of love. Thirdly, our philosophy denies the significance of each individual personality. It's easy to see that if I deny the personality of some Natalya Stepanovna, it's absolutely nothing to me whether she is insulted or not. To-day one insults her dignity as a human being and pays her *Blutgeld*, and next day thinks no more of her.

"So I sat in the summer-house and watched the young ladies. Another woman's figure appeared in the avenue, with fair hair, her head uncovered and a white knitted shawl on her shoulders. She walked along the avenue, then came into the summer-house, and taking hold of the parapet, looked indifferently below and into the distance over the sea. As she came in she paid no attention to me, as though she did not notice me. I scrutinised her from foot to head (not from head to foot, as one scrutinises men) and found that she was young, not more than five-and-twenty, nice-looking, with a good figure, in all probability married and belonging to the class of respectable women. She was dressed as though she were at home, but fashionably and with taste, as ladies are, as a rule, in N.

"'This one would do nicely,' I thought, looking at her handsome figure and her arms; 'she is all right. . . She is probably the wife of some doctor or schoolmaster. . .'

"But to make up to her—that is, to make her the heroine of one of those impromptu affairs to which tourists are so prone—was not easy and, indeed, hardly possible. I felt that as I gazed at her face. The way she looked, and the expression of her face, suggested that the sea, the smoke in the distance, and the sky had bored her long, long ago, and wearied her sight. She seemed to be tired, bored, and thinking about something dreary, and her face had not even that fussy, affectedly indifferent expression which one sees in the face of almost every woman when she is conscious of the presence of an unknown man in her vicinity.

"The fair-haired lady took a bored and passing glance at me, sat down on a seat and sank into reverie, and from her face I saw that she had no thoughts for me, and that I, with my Petersburg appearance, did not arouse in her even simple curiosity. But yet I made up my mind to speak to her, and asked: 'Madam, allow me to ask you at what time do the waggonettes go from here to the town?'

"'At ten or eleven, I believe. . .'"

"I thanked her. She glanced at me once or twice, and suddenly there was a gleam of curiosity, then of something like wonder on her passionless face. . . I made haste to assume an indifferent expression and to fall into a suitable attitude; she was catching on! She suddenly jumped up from the seat, as though something had bitten her, and examining me hurriedly, with a gentle smile, asked timidly:

"'Oh, aren't you Ananyev?'

"'Yes, I am Ananyev,' I answered.

"'And don't you recognise me? No?'

"I was a little confused. I looked intently at her, and—would you believe it?—I recognised her not from her face nor her figure, but from her gentle, weary smile. It was Natalya Stepanovna, or, as she was called, Kisotchka, the very girl I had been head over ears in love with seven or eight years before, when I was wearing the uniform of a high-school boy. The doings of far, vanished days, the days of long ago. . . I remember this Kisotchka, a thin little high-school girl of fifteen or sixteen, when she was something just for a schoolboy's taste, created by nature especially for Platonic love. What a charming little girl she was! Pale, fragile, light—she looked as though a breath would send her flying like a feather to the skies—a gentle, perplexed face, little hands, soft long hair to her belt, a waist as thin as a wasp's—altogether something ethereal, transparent like moonlight—in fact, from the point of view of a high-school boy a peerless beauty. . . Wasn't I in love with her! I did not sleep at night. I wrote verses. . . Sometimes in the evenings she would sit on a seat in the park while we schoolboys crowded round her, gazing reverently; in response to our compliments, our sighing, and attitudinising, she would shrink nervously from the evening damp, screw up her eyes, and smile gently, and at such times she was awfully like a pretty little kitten. As we gazed at her every one of us had a desire to caress her and stroke her like a cat, hence her nickname of Kisotchka.

"In the course of the seven or eight years since we had met, Kisotchka had greatly changed. She had grown more robust and stouter, and had quite lost the resemblance to a soft, fluffy kitten. It was not that her features looked old or faded, but they had somehow lost their brilliance and looked sterner, her hair seemed shorter, she looked taller, and her shoulders were quite twice as broad, and what was most striking, there was already in her face the expression of motherliness and resignation commonly seen in respectable women of her age, and this, of course, I had never seen in her before. . . In short, of the school-girlish and the Platonic her face had kept the gentle smile and nothing more. . .

"We got into conversation. Learning that I was already an engineer, Kisotchka was immensely delighted.

"'How good that is!' she said, looking joyfully into my face. 'Ah, how good! And how splendid you all are! Of all who left with you, not one has been a failure—they have all turned out well. One an engineer, another a doctor, a third a teacher, another, they say, is a celebrated singer in Petersburg. . . You are all splendid, all of you. . . Ah, how good that is!'

"Kisotchka's eyes shone with genuine goodwill and gladness. She was admiring me like an elder sister or a former governess. 'While I looked at her sweet face and thought, It wouldn't be bad to get hold of her to-day!'

"'Do you remember, Natalya Stepanovna,' I asked her, 'how I once brought you in the park a bouquet with a note in it? You read my note, and such a look of bewilderment came into your face. . .'

"'No, I don't remember that,' she said, laughing. 'But I remember how you wanted to challenge Florens to a duel over me. . .'

"'Well, would you believe it, I don't remember that. . .'

"'Well, that's all over and done with. . .' sighed Kisotchka. 'At one time I was your idol, and now it is my turn to look up to all of you. . .'

"From further conversation I learned that two years after leaving the high school, Kisotchka had been married to a resident in the town who was half Greek, half Russian, had a post either in the bank or in the insurance society, and also carried on a trade in corn. He had a strange surname, something in the style of Populaki or Skarandopulo. . . Goodness only knows—I have forgotten. . . As a matter of fact, Kisotchka spoke little and with reluctance about herself. The conversation was only about me. She asked me about the College of Engineering, about my comrades, about Petersburg, about my plans, and everything I said moved her to eager delight and exclamations of, 'Oh, how good that is!'

"We went down to the sea and walked over the sands; then when the night air began to blow chill and damp from the sea we climbed up again. All the while our talk was of me and of the past. We walked about until the reflection of the sunset had died away from the windows of the summer villas.

"'Come in and have some tea,' Kisotchka suggested. 'The samovar must have been on the table long ago. . . I am alone at home,' she said, as her villa came into sight through the green of the acacias. 'My husband is always in the town and only comes home at night, and not always then, and I must own that I am so dull that it's simply deadly.'

"I followed her in, admiring her back and shoulders. I was glad that she was married. Married women are better material for temporary love affairs than girls. I was also pleased that her husband was not at home. At the same time I felt that the affair would not come off. . .

"We went into the house. The rooms were smallish and had low ceilings, and the furniture was typical of the summer villa (Russians like having at their summer villas uncomfortable heavy, dingy furniture which they are sorry to throw away and have nowhere to put), but from certain details I could observe that Kisotchka and her husband were not badly off, and must be spending five or six thousand roubles a year. I remember that in the middle of the room which Kisotchka called the dining-room there was a round table, supported for some reason on six legs, and on it a samovar and cups. At the edge of the table lay an open book, a pencil, and an exercise book. I glanced at the book and recognised it as 'Malinin and Burenin's Arithmetical Examples.' It was open, as I now remember, at the 'Rules of Compound Interest.'

"'To whom are you giving lessons?' I asked Kisotchka.

"'Nobody,' she answered. 'I am just doing some. . . I have nothing to do, and am so bored that I think of the old days and do sums.'

"'Have you any children?'

"'I had a baby boy, but he only lived a week.'

"We began drinking tea. Admiring me, Kisotchka said again how good it was that I was an engineer, and how glad she was of my success. And the more she talked and the more genuinely she smiled, the stronger was my conviction that I should go away without having gained my object. I was a connoisseur in love affairs in those days, and could accurately gauge my chances of success. You can boldly reckon on success if you are tracking down a fool or a woman as much on the look out for new experiences and sensations as yourself, or an adventuress to whom you are a stranger. If you come across a sensible and serious woman, whose face has an expression of weary submission and goodwill, who is genuinely delighted at your presence, and, above all, respects you, you may as well turn back. To succeed in that case needs longer than one day.

"And by evening light Kisotchka seemed even more charming than by day. She attracted me more and more, and apparently she liked me too, and the surroundings were most appropriate: the husband not at home, no servants visible, stillness around. . . Though I had little confidence in success, I made up my mind to begin the attack anyway. First of all it was necessary to get into a familiar tone and to change Kisotchka's lyrically earnest mood into a more frivolous one.

"'Let us change the conversation, Natalya Stepanovna,' I began. 'Let us talk of something amusing. First of all, allow me, for the sake of old times, to call you Kisotchka.'

"She allowed me.

"'Tell me, please, Kisotchka,' I went on, 'what is the matter with all the fair sex here. What has happened to them? In old days they were all so moral and virtuous, and now, upon my word, if one asks about anyone, one is told such things that one is quite shocked at human nature. . . One young lady has eloped with an officer; another has run away and carried off a high-school boy with her; another—a married woman—has run away from her husband with an actor; a fourth has left her husband and gone off with an officer, and so on and so on. It's a regular epidemic! If it goes on like this there won't be a girl or a young woman left in your town!'

"I spoke in a vulgar, playful tone. If Kisotchka had laughed in response I should have gone on in this style: 'You had better look out, Kisotchka, or some officer or actor will be carrying you off!' She would have dropped her eyes and said: 'As though anyone would care to carry me off; there are plenty younger and better looking. . .' And I should have said: 'Nonsense, Kisotchka—I for one should be delighted!' And so on in that style, and it would all have gone swimmingly. But Kisotchka did not laugh in response; on the contrary, she looked grave and sighed.

"'All you have been told is true,' she said. 'My cousin Sonya ran away from her husband with an actor. Of course, it is wrong. . . Everyone ought to bear the lot that fate has laid on him, but I do not condemn them or blame them. . . Circumstances are sometimes too strong for anyone!'

"'That is so, Kisotchka, but what circumstances can produce a regular epidemic?'

"'It's very simple and easy to understand,' replied Kisotchka, raising her eyebrows. 'There is absolutely nothing for us educated girls and women to do with ourselves. Not everyone is able to go to the University, to become a teacher, to live for ideas, in fact, as men do. They have to be married. . . And whom would you have them marry? You boys leave the high-school and go away to the University, never to return to your native town again, and you marry in Petersburg or Moscow, while the girls remain. . . To whom are they to be married? Why, in the absence of decent cultured men, goodness knows what sort of men they marry—stockbrokers and such people of all kinds, who can do nothing but drink and get into rows at the club. . . A girl married like that, at random. . . And what is her life like afterwards? You can understand: a well-educated, cultured woman is living with a stupid, boorish man; if she meets a cultivated man, an officer, an actor, or a doctor—well, she gets to love him, her life becomes unbearable to her, and she runs away from her husband. And one can't condemn her!'

"'If that is so, Kisotchka, why get married?' I asked.

"'Yes, of course,' said Kisotchka with a sigh, 'but you know every girl fancies that any husband is better than nothing. . . Altogether life is horrid here, Nikolay Anastasyevitch, very horrid! Life is stifling for a girl and stifling when one is married. . . Here they laugh at Sonya for having run away from her husband, but if they could see into her soul they would not laugh. . .'"

Azorka began barking outside again. He growled angrily at some one, then howled miserably and dashed with all his force against the wall of the hut. . . Ananyev's face was puckered with pity; he broke off his story and went out. For two minutes he could be heard outside comforting his dog. "Good dog! poor dog!"

"Our Nikolay Anastasyevitch is fond of talking," said Von Schtenberg, laughing. "He is a good fellow," he added after a brief silence.

Returning to the hut, the engineer filled up our glasses and, smiling and stroking his chest, went on:

"And so my attack was unsuccessful. There was nothing for it, I put off my unclean thoughts to a more favourable occasion, resigned myself to my failure and, as the saying is, waved my hand. What is more, under the influence of Kisotchka's voice, the evening air, and the stillness, I gradually myself fell into a quiet sentimental mood. I remember I sat in an easy chair by the wide-open window and glanced at the trees and darkened sky. The outlines of the acacias and the lime trees were just the same as they had been eight years before; just as then, in the days of my childhood, somewhere far away there was the tinkling of a wretched piano, and the public had just the same habit of sauntering to and fro along the avenues, but the people were not the same. Along the avenues there walked now not my comrades and I and the object of my adoration, but schoolboys and young ladies who were strangers. And I felt melancholy. When to my inquiries about acquaintances I five times received from Kisotchka the answer, 'He is dead,' my melancholy changed into the feeling one has at the funeral service of a good man. And sitting there at the window, looking at the promenading public and listening to the tinkling piano, I saw with my own eyes for the first time in my life with what eagerness one generation hastens to replace another, and what a momentous significance even some seven or eight years may have in a man's life!

"Kisotchka put a bottle of red wine on the table. I drank it off, grew sentimental, and began telling a long story about something or other. Kisotchka listened as before, admiring me and my cleverness. And time passed. The sky was by now so dark that the outlines of the acacias and lime trees melted into one, the public was no longer walking up and down the avenues, the piano was silent and the only sound was the even murmur of the sea.

"Young people are all alike. Be friendly to a young man, make much of him, regale him with wine, let him understand that he is attractive and he will sit on and on, forget that it is time to go, and talk and talk and talk. . . His hosts cannot keep their eyes open, it's past their bedtime, and he still stays and talks. That was what I did. Once I chanced to look at the clock; it was half-past ten. I began saying good-bye.

"'Have another glass before your walk,' said Kisotchka.

"I took another glass, again I began talking at length, forgot it was time to go, and sat down. Then there came the sound of men's voices, footsteps and the clank of spurs.

"'I think my husband has come in. . .' said Kisotchka listening.

"The door creaked, two voices came now from the passage and I saw two men pass the door that led into the dining-room: one a stout, solid, dark man with a hooked nose, wearing a straw hat, and the other a young officer in a white tunic. As they passed the door they both glanced casually and indifferently at Kisotchka and me, and I fancied both of them were drunk.

"'She told you a lie then, and you believed her!' we heard a loud voice with a marked nasal twang say a minute later. 'To begin with, it wasn't at the big club but at the little one.'

"'You are angry, Jupiter, so you are wrong. . .' said another voice, obviously the officer's, laughing and coughing. 'I say, can I stay the night? Tell me honestly, shall I be in your way?'

"'What a question! Not only you can, but you must. What will you have, beer or wine?'

"They were sitting two rooms away from us, talking loudly, and apparently feeling no interest in Kisotchka or her visitor. A perceptible change came over Kisotchka on her husband's arrival. At first she flushed red, then her face wore a timid, guilty expression; she seemed to be troubled by some anxiety, and I began to fancy that she was ashamed to show me her husband and wanted me to go.

"I began taking leave. Kisotchka saw me to the front door. I remember well her gentle mournful smile and kind patient eyes as she pressed my hand and said:

"'Most likely we shall never see each other again. Well, God give you every blessing. Thank you!'

"Not one sigh, not one fine phrase. As she said good-bye she was holding the candle in her hand; patches of light danced over her face and neck, as though chasing her mournful smile. I pictured to myself the old Kisotchka whom one used to want to stroke like a cat, I looked intently at the present Kisotchka, and for some reason recalled her words: 'Everyone ought to bear the lot that fate has laid on him.' And I had a pang at my heart. I instinctively guessed how it was, and my conscience whispered to me that I, in my happiness and indifference, was face to face with a good, warm-hearted, loving creature, who was broken by suffering.

"I said good-bye and went to the gate. By now it was quite dark. In the south the evenings draw in early in July and it gets dark rapidly. Towards ten o'clock it is so dark that you can't see an inch before your nose. I lighted a couple of dozen matches before, almost groping, I found my way to the gate.

"'Cab!' I shouted, going out of the gate; not a sound, not a sigh in answer. . . 'Cab,' I repeated, 'hey, Cab!'

"But there was no cab of any description. The silence of the grave. I could hear nothing but the murmur of the drowsy sea and the beating of my heart from the wine. Lifting my eyes to the sky I found not a single star. It was dark and sullen. Evidently the sky was covered with clouds. For some reason I shrugged my shoulders, smiling foolishly, and once more, not quite so resolutely, shouted for a cab.

"The echo answered me. A walk of three miles across open country and in the pitch dark was not an agreeable prospect. Before making up my mind to walk, I spent a long time deliberating and shouting for a cab; then, shrugging my shoulders, I walked lazily back to the copse, with no definite object in my mind. It was dreadfully dark in the copse. Here and there between the trees the windows of the summer villas glowed a dull red. A raven, disturbed by my steps and the matches with which I lighted my way to the summer-house, flew from tree to tree and rustled among the leaves. I felt vexed and ashamed, and the raven seemed to understand this, and croaked 'krrra!' I was vexed that I had to walk, and ashamed that I had stayed on at Kisotchka's, chatting like a boy.

"I made my way to the summer-house, felt for the seat and sat down. Far below me, behind a veil of thick darkness, the sea kept up a low angry growl. I remember that, as though I were blind, I could see neither sky nor sea, nor even the summer-house in which I was sitting. And it seemed to me as though the whole world consisted only of the thoughts that were straying through my head, dizzy from the wine, and of an unseen power murmuring monotonously somewhere below. And afterwards, as I sank into a doze, it began to seem that it was not the sea murmuring, but my thoughts, and that the whole world consisted of nothing but me. And concentrating the whole world in myself in this way, I thought no more of cabs, of the town, and of Kisotchka, and abandoned myself to the sensation I was so fond of: that is, the sensation of fearful isolation when you feel that in the whole universe, dark and formless, you alone exist. It is a proud, demoniac sensation, only possible to Russians whose thoughts and sensations are as large, boundless, and gloomy as their plains, their forests, and their snow. If I had been an artist I should certainly have depicted the expression of a Russian's face when he sits motionless and, with his legs under him and his head clasped in his hands, abandons himself to this sensation. . . And together with this sensation come thoughts of the aimlessness of life, of death, and of the darkness of the grave. . . The thoughts are not worth a brass farthing, but the expression of face must be fine. . .

"While I was sitting and dozing, unable to bring myself to get up—I was warm and comfortable—all at once, against the even monotonous murmur of the sea, as though upon a canvas, sounds began to grow distinct which drew my attention from myself. . . Someone was coming hurriedly along the avenue. Reaching the summer-house this someone stopped, gave a sob like a little girl, and said in the voice of a weeping child: 'My God, when will it all end! Merciful Heavens!'

"Judging from the voice and the weeping I took it to be a little girl of ten or twelve. She walked irresolutely into the summer-house, sat down, and began half-praying, half-complaining aloud. . .

"'Merciful God!' she said, crying, 'it's unbearable. It's beyond all endurance! I suffer in silence, but I want to live too. . . Oh, my God! My God!'

"And so on in the same style.

"I wanted to look at the child and speak to her. So as not to frighten her I first gave a loud sigh and coughed, then cautiously struck a match. . . There was a flash of bright light in the darkness, which lighted up the weeping figure. It was Kisotchka!"

"Marvels upon marvels!" said Von Schtenberg with a sigh. "Black night, the murmur of the sea; she in grief, he with a sensation of world—solitude. . . It's too much of a good thing. . . You only want Circassians with daggers to complete it."

"I am not telling you a tale, but fact."

"Well, even if it is a fact. . . it all proves nothing, and there is nothing new in it. . ."

"Wait a little before you find fault! Let me finish," said Ananyev, waving his hand with vexation; "don't interfere, please! I am not telling you, but the doctor. . . Well," he went on, addressing me and glancing askance at the student who bent over his books and seemed very well satisfied at having gibed at the engineer—"well, Kisotchka was not surprised or frightened at seeing me. It seemed as though she had known beforehand that she would find me in the summer-house. She was breathing in gasps and trembling all over as though in a fever, while her tear-stained face, so far as I could distinguish it as I struck match after match, was not the intelligent, submissive weary face I had seen before, but something different, which I cannot understand to this day. It did not express pain, nor anxiety, nor misery—nothing of what was expressed by her words and her tears. . . I must own that, probably because I did not understand it, it looked to me senseless and as though she were drunk.

"'I can't bear it,' muttered Kisotchka in the voice of a crying child. 'It's too much for me, Nikolay Anastasyitch. Forgive me, Nikolav Anastasyitch. I can't go on living like this. . . I am going to the town to my mother's. . . Take me there. . . Take me there, for God's sake!'

"In the presence of tears I can neither speak nor be silent. I was flustered and muttered some nonsense trying to comfort her.

"'No, no; I will go to my mother's,' said Kisotchka resolutely, getting up and clutching my arm convulsively (her hands and her sleeves were wet with tears). 'Forgive me, Nikolay Anastasyitch, I am going. . . I can bear no more. . .'

"'Kisotchka, but there isn't a single cab,' I said. 'How can you go?'

"'No matter, I'll walk. . . It's not far. I can't bear it. . .'

"I was embarrassed, but not touched. Kisotchka's tears, her trembling, and the blank expression of her face suggested to me a trivial, French or Little Russian melodrama, in which every ounce of cheap shallow feeling is washed down with pints of tears.

"I didn t understand her, and knew I did not understand her; I ought to have been silent, but for some reason, most likely for fear my silence might be taken for stupidity, I thought fit to try to persuade her not to go to her mother's, but to stay at home. When people cry, they don't like their tears to be seen. And I lighted match after match and went on striking till the box was empty. What I wanted with this ungenerous illumination, I can't conceive to this day. Cold-hearted people are apt to be awkward, and even stupid.

"In the end Kisotchka took my arm and we set off. Going out of the gate, we turned to the right and sauntered slowly along the soft dusty road. It was dark. As my eyes grew gradually accustomed to the darkness, I began to distinguish the silhouettes of the old gaunt oaks and lime trees which bordered the road. The jagged, precipitous cliffs, intersected here and there by deep, narrow ravines and creeks, soon showed indistinctly, a black streak on the right. Low bushes nestled by the hollows, looking like sitting figures. It was uncanny. I looked sideways suspiciously at the cliffs, and the murmur of the sea and the stillness of the country alarmed my imagination. Kisotchka did not speak. She was still trembling, and before she had gone half a mile she was exhausted with walking and was out of breath. I too was silent.

"Three-quarters of a mile from the Quarantine Station there was a deserted building of four storeys, with a very high chimney in which there had once been a steam flour mill. It stood solitary on the cliff, and by day it could be seen for a long distance, both by sea and by land. Because it was deserted and no one lived in it, and because there was an echo in it which distinctly repeated the steps and voices of passers-by, it seemed mysterious. Picture me in the dark night arm-in-arm with a woman who was running away from her husband near this tall long monster which repeated the sound of every step I took and stared at me fixedly with its hundred black windows. A normal young man would have been moved to romantic feelings in such surroundings, but I looked at the dark windows and thought: 'All this is very impressive, but time will come when of that building and of Kisotchka and her troubles and of me with my thoughts, not one grain of dust will remain. . . All is nonsense and vanity. . .'

"When we reached the flour mill Kisotchka suddenly stopped, took her arm out of mine, and said, no longer in a childish voice, but in her own:

"'Nikolay Anastasvitch, I know all this seems strange to you. But I am terribly unhappy! And you cannot even imagine how unhappy! It's impossible to imagine it! I don't tell you about it because one can't talk about it. . . Such a life, such a life! . . .'

"Kisotchka did not finish. She clenched her teeth and moaned as though she were doing her utmost not to scream with pain.

"'Such a life!' she repeated with horror, with the cadence and the southern, rather Ukrainian accent which particularly in women gives to emotional speech the effect of singing. 'It is a life! Ah, my God, my God! what does it mean? Oh, my God, my God!'

"As though trying to solve the riddle of her fate, she shrugged her shoulders in perplexity, shook her head, and clasped her hands. She spoke as though she were singing, moved gracefully, and reminded me of a celebrated Little Russian actress.

"'Great God, it is as though I were in a pit,' she went on. 'If one could

34   ANTON CHEKHOV

live for one minute in happiness as other people live! Oh, my God, my God! I have come to such disgrace that before a stranger I am running away from my husband by night, like some disreputable creature! Can I expect anything good after that?'

"As I admired her movements and her voice, I began to feel annoyed that she was not on good terms with her husband. 'It would be nice to have got on into relations with her!' flitted through my mind; and this pitiless thought stayed in my brain, haunted me all the way and grew more and more alluring.

"About a mile from the flour mill we had to turn to the left by the cemetery. At the turning by the corner of the cemetery there stood a stone windmill, and by it a little hut in which the miller lived. We passed the mill and the hut, turned to the left and reached the gates of the cemetery. There Kisotchka stopped and said:

"'I am going back, Nikolay Anastasyitch! You go home, and God bless you, but I am going back. I am not frightened.'

"'Well, what next!' I said, disconcerted. 'If you are going, you had better go!'

"'I have been too hasty. . . It was all about nothing that mattered. You and your talk took me back to the past and put all sort of ideas into my head. . . I was sad and wanted to cry, and my husband said rude things to me before that officer, and I could not bear it. . . And what's the good of my going to the town to my mother's? Will that make me any happier? I must go back. . . But never mind. . . let us go on,' said Kisotchka, and she laughed. 'It makes no difference!'

"I remembered that over the gate of the cemetery there was an inscription: 'The hour will come wherein all they that lie in the grave will hear the voice of the Son of God.' I knew very well that sooner or later I and Kisotchka and her husband and the officer in the white tunic would lie under the dark trees in the churchyard; I knew that an unhappy and insulted fellow-creature was walking beside me. All this I recognised distinctly, but at the same time I was troubled by an oppressive and unpleasant dread that Kisotchka would turn back, and that I should not manage to say to her what had to be said. Never at any other time in my life have thoughts of a higher order been so closely interwoven with the basest animal prose as on that night. . . It was horrible!

"Not far from the cemetery we found a cab. When we reached the High Street, where Kisotchka's mother lived, we dismissed the cab and walked along the pavement. Kisotchka was silent all the while, while I looked at her, and I raged at myself, 'Why don't you begin? Now's the time!' About twenty paces from the hotel where I was staying, Kisotchka stopped by the lamp-post and burst into tears.

"'Nikolay Anastasyitch!' she said, crying and laughing and looking at me with wet shining eyes, 'I shall never forget your sympathy. . . How good you are! All of you are so splendid—all of you! Honest, great-hearted, kind, clever. . . Ah, how good that is!'

"She saw in me a highly educated man, advanced in every sense of the word, and on her tear-stained laughing face, together with the emotion and enthusiasm aroused by my personality, there was clearly written regret that she so rarely saw such people, and that God had not vouchsafed her the bliss of being the wife of one of them. She muttered, 'Ah, how splendid it is!' The childish gladness on her face, the tears, the gentle smile, the soft hair, which had escaped from under the kerchief, and the kerchief itself thrown carelessly over her head, in the light of the street lamp reminded me of the old Kisotchka whom one had wanted to stroke like a kitten.

"I could not restrain myself, and began stroking her hair, her shoulders, and her hands.

"'Kisotchka, what do you want?' I muttered. 'I'll go to the ends of the earth with you if you like! I will take you out of this hole and give you happiness. I love you. . . Let us go, my sweet? Yes? Will you?'

"Kisotchka's face was flooded with bewilderment. She stepped back from the street lamp and, completely overwhelmed, gazed at me with wide-open eyes. I gripped her by the arm, began showering kisses on her face, her neck, her shoulders, and went on making vows and promises. In love affairs vows and promises are almost a physiological necessity. There's no getting on without them. Sometimes you know you are lying and that promises are not necessary, but still you vow and protest. Kisotchka, utterly overwhelmed, kept staggering back and gazing at me with round eyes.

"'Please don't! Please don't!' she muttered, holding me off with her hands.

"I clasped her tightly in my arms. All at once she broke into hysterical tears. And her face had the same senseless blank expression that I had seen in the summer-house when I lighted the matches. Without asking her consent, preventing her from speaking, I dragged her forcibly towards my hotel. She seemed almost swooning and did not walk, but

I took her under the arms and almost carried her. . . I remember, as we were going up the stairs, some man with a red band in his cap looked wonderingly at me and bowed to Kisotchka. . ."

Ananyev flushed crimson and paused. He walked up and down near the table in silence, scratched the back of his head with an air of vexation, and several times shrugged his shoulders and twitched his shoulder-blades, while a shiver ran down his huge back. The memory was painful and made him ashamed, and he was struggling with himself.

"It's horrible!" he said, draining a glass of wine and shaking his head. "I am told that in every introductory lecture on women's diseases the medical students are admonished to remember that each one of them has a mother, a sister, a fiancée, before undressing and examining a female patient. . . That advice would be very good not only for medical students but for everyone who in one way or another has to deal with a woman's life. Now that I have a wife and a little daughter, oh, how well I understand that advice! How I understand it, my God! You may as well hear the rest, though. . . As soon as she had become my mistress, Kisotchka's view of the position was very different from mine. First of all she felt for me a deep and passionate love. What was for me an ordinary amatory episode was for her an absolute revolution in her life. I remember, it seemed to me that she had gone out of her mind. Happy for the first time in her life, looking five years younger, with an inspired enthusiastic face, not knowing what to do with herself for happiness, she laughed and cried and never ceased dreaming aloud how next day we would set off for the Caucasus, then in the autumn to Petersburg; how we would live afterwards.

"'Don't worry yourself about my husband,' she said to reassure me. 'He is bound to give me a divorce. Everyone in the town knows that he is living with the elder Kostovitch. We will get a divorce and be married.'

"When women love they become acclimatised and at home with people very quickly, like cats. Kisotchka had only spent an hour and a half in my room when she already felt as though she were at home and was ready to treat my property as though it were her own. She packed my things in my portmanteau, scolded me for not hanging my new expensive overcoat on a peg instead of flinging it on a chair, and so on.

"I looked at her, listened, and felt weariness and vexation. I was conscious of a slight twinge of horror at the thought that a respectable, honest, and unhappy woman had so easily, after some three or four hours, succumbed to the first man she met. As a respectable man, you see, I didn't like it. Then, too, I was unpleasantly impressed by the fact that women of Kisotchka's sort, not deep or serious, are too much in love with life, and exalt what is in reality such a trifle as love for a man to the level of bliss, misery, a complete revolution in life. . . Moreover, now that I was satisfied, I was vexed with myself for having been so stupid as to get entangled with a woman whom I should have to deceive. And in spite of my disorderly life I must observe that I could not bear telling lies.

"I remember that Kisotchka sat down at my feet, laid her head on my knees, and, looking at me with shining, loving eyes, asked:

"'Kolya, do you love me? Very, very much?'

"And she laughed with happiness. . . This struck me as sentimental, affected, and not clever; and meanwhile I was already inclined to look for 'depth of thought' before everything.

"'Kisotchka, you had better go home,' I said, or else your people will be sure to miss you and will be looking for you all over the town; and it would be awkward for you to go to your mother in the morning.'

"Kisotchka agreed. At parting we arranged to meet at midday next morning in the park, and the day after to set off together to Pyatigorsk. I went into the street to see her home, and I remember that I caressed her with genuine tenderness on the way. There was a minute when I felt unbearably sorry for her, for trusting me so implicitly, and I made up my mind that I would really take her to Pyatigorsk, but remembering that I had only six hundred roubles in my portmanteau, and that it would be far more difficult to break it off with her in the autumn than now, I made haste to suppress my compassion.

"We reached the house where Kisotchka's mother lived. I pulled at the bell. When footsteps were heard at the other side of the door Kisotchka suddenly looked grave, glanced upwards to the sky, made the sign of the Cross over me several times and, clutching my hand, pressed it to her lips.

"'Till to-morrow,' she said, and disappeared into the house.

"I crossed to the opposite pavement and from there looked at the house. At first the windows were in darkness, then in one of the windows there was the glimmer of the faint bluish flame of a newly lighted candle; the flame grew, gave more light, and I saw shadows moving about the rooms together with it.

"'They did not expect her,' I thought.

"Returning to my hotel room I undressed, drank off a glass of red wine, ate some fresh caviare which I had bought that day in the bazaar, went to bed in a leisurely way, and slept the sound, untroubled sleep of a tourist.

"In the morning I woke up with a headache and in a bad humour. Something worried me.

"'What's the matter?' I asked myself, trying to explain my uneasiness. 'What's upsetting me?'

"And I put down my uneasiness to the dread that Kisotchka might turn up any minute and prevent my going away, and that I should have to tell lies and act a part before her. I hurriedly dressed, packed my things, and left the hotel, giving instructions to the porter to take my luggage to the station for the seven o'clock train in the evening. I spent the whole day with a doctor friend and left the town that evening. As you see, my philosophy did not prevent me from taking to my heels in a mean and treacherous flight. . .

"All the while that I was at my friend's, and afterwards driving to the station, I was tormented by anxiety. I fancied that I was afraid of meeting with Kisotchka and a scene. In the station I purposely remained in the toilet room till the second bell rang, and while I was making my way to my compartment, I was oppressed by a feeling as though I were covered all over with stolen things. With what impatience and terror I waited for the third bell!

"At last the third bell that brought my deliverance rang at last, the train moved; we passed the prison, the barracks, came out into the open country, and yet, to my surprise, the feeling of uneasiness still persisted, and still I felt like a thief passionately longing to escape. It was queer. To distract my mind and calm myself I looked out of the window. The train ran along the coast. The sea was smooth, and the turquoise sky, almost half covered with the tender, golden crimson light of sunset, was gaily and serenely mirrored in it. Here and there fishing boats and rafts made black patches on its surface. The town, as clean and beautiful as a toy, stood on the high cliff, and was already shrouded in the mist of evening. The golden domes of its churches, the windows and the greenery reflected the setting sun, glowing and melting like shimmering gold. . . The scent of the fields mingled with the soft damp air from the sea.

"The train flew rapidly along. I heard the laughter of passengers and guards. Everyone was good-humoured and light-hearted, yet my unaccountable uneasiness grew greater and greater. . . I looked at the white mist that covered the town and I imagined how a woman with a senseless blank face was hurrying up and down in that mist by the churches and the houses, looking for me and moaning, 'Oh, my God! Oh, my God!' in the voice of a little girl or the cadences of a Little Russian actress. I recalled her grave face and big anxious eyes as she made the sign of the Cross over me, as though I belonged to her, and mechanically I looked at the hand which she had kissed the day before.

"'Surely I am not in love?' I asked myself, scratching my hand.

"Only as night came on when the passengers were asleep and I was left *tête-à-tête* with my conscience, I began to understand what I had not been able to grasp before. In the twilight of the railway carriage the image of Kisotchka rose before me, haunted me and I recognised clearly that I had committed a crime as bad as murder. My conscience tormented me. To stifle this unbearable feeling, I assured myself that everything was nonsense and vanity, that Kisotchka and I would die and decay, that her grief was nothing in comparison with death, and so on and so on. . . and that if you come to that, there is no such thing as freewill, and that therefore I was not to blame. But all these arguments only irritated me and were extraordinarily quickly crowded out by other thoughts. There was a miserable feeling in the hand that Kisotchka had kissed. . . I kept lying down and getting up again, drank vodka at the stations, forced myself to eat bread and butter, fell to assuring myself again that life had no meaning, but nothing was of any use. A strange and if you like absurd ferment was going on in my brain. The most incongruous ideas crowded one after another in disorder, getting more and more tangled, thwarting each other, and I, the thinker, 'with my brow bent on the earth,' could make out nothing and could not find my bearings in this mass of essential and non-essential ideas. It appeared that I, the thinker, had not mastered the technique of thinking, and that I was no more capable of managing my own brain than mending a watch. For the first time in my life I was really thinking eagerly and intensely, and that seemed to me so monstrous that I said to myself: 'I am going off my head.' A man whose brain does not work at all times, but only at painful moments, is often haunted by the thought of madness.

"I spent a day and a night in this misery, then a second night, and learning from experience how little my philosophy was to me, I came to my senses and realised at last what sort of a creature I was. I saw that my ideas were not worth a brass farthing, and that before meeting Kisotchka I had not begun to think and had not even a conception of what thinking in earnest meant; now through suffering I realised that I had neither convictions nor a definite moral standard, nor heart, nor reason; my whole intellectual and moral wealth consisted of specialist knowledge, fragments, useless memories, other people's ideas—and nothing else; and my mental processes were as lacking in complexity, as useless and as rudimentary as a Yakut's. . . If I had disliked lying, had not stolen, had not murdered, and, in fact, made obviously gross mistakes, that was not owing to my convictions—I had none, but because I was in bondage, hand and foot, to my nurse's fairy tales and to copy-book morals, which had entered into my flesh and blood and without my noticing it guided me in life, though I looked on them as absurd. . .

"I realised that I was not a thinker, not a philosopher, but simply a dilettante. God had given me a strong healthy Russian brain with promise of talent. And, only fancy, here was that brain at twenty-six, undisciplined, completely free from principles, not weighed down by any stores of knowledge, but only lightly sprinkled with information of a sort in the engineering line; it was young and had a physiological craving for exercise, it was on the look-out for it, when all at once quite casually the fine juicy idea of the aimlessness of life and the darkness beyond the tomb descends upon it. It greedily sucks it in, puts its whole outlook at its disposal and begins playing with it, like a cat with a mouse. There is neither learning nor system in the brain, but that does not matter. It deals with the great ideas with its own innate powers, like a self-educated man, and before a month has passed the owner of the brain can turn a potato into a hundred dainty dishes, and fancies himself a philosopher. . .

"Our generation has carried this dilettantism, this playing with serious ideas into science, into literature, into politics, and into everything which it is not too lazy to go into, and with its dilettantism has introduced, too, its coldness, its boredom, and its one-sidedness and, as it seems to me, it has already succeeded in developing in the masses a new hitherto non-existent attitude to serious ideas.

"I realised and appreciated my abnormality and utter ignorance, thanks to a misfortune. My normal thinking, so it seems to me now, dates from the day when I began again from the A, B, C, when my conscience sent me flying back to N., when with no philosophical subleties I repented, besought Kisotchka's forgiveness like a naughty boy and wept with her. . ."

Ananyev briefly described his last interview with Kisotchka.

"H'm. . ." the student filtered through his teeth when the engineer had finished. "That's the sort of thing that happens."

His face still expressed mental inertia, and apparently Ananyev's story had not touched him in the least. Only when the engineer after a moment's pause, began expounding his view again and repeating what he had said at first, the student frowned irritably, got up from the table and walked away to his bed. He made his bed and began undressing.

"You look as though you have really convinced some one this time," he said irritably.

"Me convince anybody!" said the engineer. "My dear soul, do you suppose I claim to do that? God bless you! To convince you is impossible. You can reach conviction only by way of personal experience and suffering!"

"And then—it's queer logic!" grumbled the student as he put on his nightshirt. "The ideas which you so dislike, which are so ruinous for the young are, according to you, the normal thing for the old; it's as though it were a question of grey hairs. . . Where do the old get this privilege? What is it based upon? If these ideas are poison, they are equally poisonous for all?"

"Oh, no, my dear soul, don't say so!" said the engineer with a sly wink. "Don't say so. In the first place, old men are not dilettanti. Their pessimism comes to them not casually from outside, but from the depths of their own brains, and only after they have exhaustively studied the Hegels and Kants of all sorts, have suffered, have made no end of mistakes, in fact—when they have climbed the whole ladder from bottom to top. Their pessimism has both personal experience and sound philosophic training behind it. Secondly, the pessimism of old thinkers does not take the form of idle talk, as it does with you and me, but of *Weltschmertz*, of suffering; it rests in them on a Christian foundation because it is derived from love for humanity and from thoughts about humanity, and is entirely free from the egoism which is noticeable in dilettanti. You despise life because its meaning and its object are hidden just from you, and you are only afraid of your own death, while the real thinker is unhappy because the truth is hidden from all and he is afraid for all men. For instance, there is living not far from here the Crown forester, Ivan Alexandritch. He is a nice old man. At one time he was a teacher

ANTON CHEKHOV

somewhere, and used to write something; the devil only knows what he was, but anyway he is a remarkably clever fellow and in philosophy he is A1. He has read a great deal and he is continually reading now. Well, we came across him lately in the Gruzovsky district. . . They were laying the sleepers and rails just at the time. It's not a difficult job, but Ivan Alexandritch, not being a specialist, looked at it as though it were a conjuring trick. It takes an experienced workman less than a minute to lay a sleeper and fix a rail on it. The workmen were in good form and really were working smartly and rapidly; one rascal in particular brought his hammer down with exceptional smartness on the head of the nail and drove it in at one blow, though the handle of the hammer was two yards or more in length and each nail was a foot long. Ivan Alexandritch watched the workmen a long time, was moved, and said to me with tears in his eyes:

"'What a pity that these splendid men will die!' Such pessimism I understand."

"All that proves nothing and explains nothing," said the student, covering himself up with a sheet; "all that is simply pounding liquid in a mortar. No one knows anything and nothing can be proved by words."

He peeped out from under the sheet, lifted up his head and, frowning irritably, said quickly:

"One must be very naïve to believe in human words and logic and to ascribe any determining value to them. You can prove and disprove anything you like with words, and people will soon perfect the technique of language to such a point that they will prove with mathematical certainty that twice two is seven. I am fond of reading and listening, but as to believing, no thank you; I can't, and I don't want to. I believe only in God, but as for you, if you talk to me till the Second Coming and seduce another five hundred Kisothchkas, I shall believe in you only when I go out of my mind. . . Goodnight."

The student hid his head under the sheet and turned his face towards the wall, meaning by this action to let us know that he did not want to speak or listen. The argument ended at that.

Before going to bed the engineer and I went out of the hut, and I saw the lights once more.

"We have tired you out with our chatter," said Ananyev, yawning and looking at the sky. "Well, my good sir! The only pleasure we have in this dull hole is drinking and philosophising. . . What an embankment,

Lord have mercy on us!" he said admiringly, as we approached the embankment; "it is more like Mount Ararat than an embankment."

He paused for a little, then said: "Those lights remind the Baron of the Amalekites, but it seems to me that they are like the thoughts of man... You know the thoughts of each individual man are scattered like that in disorder, stretch in a straight line towards some goal in the midst of the darkness and, without shedding light on anything, without lighting up the night, they vanish somewhere far beyond old age. But enough philosophising! It's time to go bye-bye."

When we were back in the hut the engineer began begging me to take his bed.

"Oh please!" he said imploringly, pressing both hands on his heart. "I entreat you, and don't worry about me! I can sleep anywhere, and, besides, I am not going to bed just yet. Please do—it's a favour!"

I agreed, undressed, and went to bed, while he sat down to the table and set to work on the plans.

"We fellows have no time for sleep," he said in a low voice when I had got into bed and shut my eyes. "When a man has a wife and two children he can't think of sleep. One must think now of food and clothes and saving for the future. And I have two of them, a little son and a daughter... The boy, little rascal, has a jolly little face. He's not six yet, and already he shows remarkable abilities, I assure you... I have their photographs here, somewhere... Ah, my children, my children!"

He rummaged among his papers, found their photographs, and began looking at them. I fell asleep.

I was awakened by the barking of Azorka and loud voices. Von Schtenberg with bare feet and ruffled hair was standing in the doorway dressed in his underclothes, talking loudly with some one... It was getting light. A gloomy dark blue dawn was peeping in at the door, at the windows, and through the crevices in the hut walls, and casting a faint light on my bed, on the table with the papers, and on Ananyev. Stretched on the floor on a cloak, with a leather pillow under his head, the engineer lay asleep with his fleshy, hairy chest uppermost; he was snoring so loudly that I pitied the student from the bottom of my heart for having to sleep in the same room with him every night.

"Why on earth are we to take them?" shouted Von Schtenberg. "It has nothing to do with us! Go to Tchalisov! From whom do the cauldrons come?"

"From Nikitin..." a bass voice answered gruffly.

"Well, then, take them to Tchalisov. . . That's not in our department. What the devil are you standing there for? Drive on!"

"Your honour, we have been to Tchalisov already," said the bass voice still more gruffly. "Yesterday we were the whole day looking for him down the line, and were told at his hut that he had gone to the Dymkovsky section. Please take them, your honour! How much longer are we to go carting them about? We go carting them on and on along the line, and see no end to it."

"What is it?" Ananyev asked huskily, waking up and lifting his head quickly.

"They have brought some cauldrons from Nikitin's," said the student, "and he is begging us to take them. And what business is it of ours to take them?"

"Do be so kind, your honour, and set things right! The horses have been two days without food and the master, for sure, will be angry. Are we to take them back, or what? The railway ordered the cauldrons, so it ought to take them. . ."

"Can't you understand, you blockhead, that it has nothing to do with us? Go on to Tchalisov!"

"What is it? Who's there?" Ananyev asked huskily again. "Damnation take them all," he said, getting up and going to the door. "What is it?"

I dressed, and two minutes later went out of the hut. Ananyev and the student, both in their underclothes and barefooted, were angrily and impatiently explaining to a peasant who was standing before them bare-headed, with his whip in his hand, apparently not understanding them. Both faces looked preoccupied with workaday cares.

"What use are your cauldrons to me," shouted Ananyev. "Am I to put them on my head, or what? If you can't find Tchalisov, find his assistant, and leave us in peace!"

Seeing me, the student probably recalled the conversation of the previous night. The workaday expression vanished from his sleepy face and a look of mental inertia came into it. He waved the peasant off and walked away absorbed in thought.

It was a cloudy morning. On the line where the lights had been gleaming the night before, the workmen, just roused from sleep, were swarming. There was a sound of voices and the squeaking of wheelbarrows. The working day was beginning. One poor little nag harnessed with cord was already plodding towards the embankment, tugging with its neck, and dragging along a cartful of sand.

I began saying good-bye. . . A great deal had been said in the night, but I carried away with me no answer to any question, and in the morning, of the whole conversation there remained in my memory, as in a filter, only the lights and the image of Kisotchka. As I got on the horse, I looked at the student and Ananyev for the last time, at the hysterical dog with the lustreless, tipsy-looking eyes, at the workmen flitting to and fro in the morning fog, at the embankment, at the little nag straining with its neck, and thought:

"There is no making out anything in this world."

And when I lashed my horse and galloped along the line, and when a little later I saw nothing before me but the endless gloomy plain and the cold overcast sky, I recalled the questions which were discussed in the night. I pondered while the sun-scorched plain, the immense sky, the oak forest, dark on the horizon and the hazy distance, seemed saying to me:

"Yes, there's no understanding anything in this world!"

The sun began to rise. . .

A Story without an End

S oon after two o'clock one night, long ago, the cook, pale and agitated, rushed unexpectedly into my study and informed me that Madame Mimotih, the old woman who owned the house next door, was sitting in her kitchen.

"She begs you to go in to her, sir. . ." said the cook, panting. "Something bad has happened about her lodger. . . He has shot himself or hanged himself. . ."

"What can I do?" said I. "Let her go for the doctor or for the police!"

"How is she to look for a doctor! She can hardly breathe, and she has huddled under the stove, she is so frightened. . . You had better go round, sir."

I put on my coat and hat and went to Madame Mimotih's house. The gate towards which I directed my steps was open. After pausing beside it, uncertain what to do, I went into the yard without feeling for the porter's bell. In the dark and dilapidated porch the door was not locked. I opened it and walked into the entry. Here there was not a glimmer of light, it was pitch dark, and, moreover, there was a marked smell of incense. Groping my way out of the entry I knocked my elbow against something made of iron, and in the darkness stumbled against a board of some sort which almost fell to the floor. At last the door covered with torn baize was found, and I went into a little hall.

I am not at the moment writing a fairy tale, and am far from intending to alarm the reader, but the picture I saw from the passage was fantastic and could only have been drawn by death. Straight before me was a door leading to a little drawing-room. Three five-kopeck wax candles, standing in a row, threw a scanty light on the faded slate-coloured wallpaper. A coffin was standing on two tables in the middle of the little room. The two candles served only to light up a swarthy yellow face with a half-open mouth and sharp nose. Billows of muslin were mingled in disorder from the face to the tips of the two shoes, and from among the billows peeped out two pale motionless hands, holding a wax cross. The dark gloomy corners of the little drawing-room, the ikons behind the coffin, the coffin itself, everything except the softly glimmering lights, were still as death, as the tomb itself.

"How strange!" I thought, dumbfounded by the unexpected panorama of death. "Why this haste? The lodger has hardly had time to hang himself, or shoot himself, and here is the coffin already!"

I looked round. On the left there was a door with a glass panel; on the right a lame hat-stand with a shabby fur coat on it. . .

"Water. . ." I heard a moan.

The moan came from the left, beyond the door with the glass panel. I opened the door and walked into a little dark room with a solitary window, through which there came a faint light from a street lamp outside.

"Is anyone here?" I asked.

And without waiting for an answer I struck a match. This is what I saw while it was burning. A man was sitting on the blood-stained floor at my very feet. If my step had been a longer one I should have trodden on him. With his legs thrust forward and his hands pressed on the floor, he was making an effort to raise his handsome face, which was deathly pale against his pitch-black beard. In the big eyes which he lifted upon me, I read unutterable terror, pain, and entreaty. A cold sweat trickled in big drops down his face. That sweat, the expression of his face, the trembling of the hands he leaned upon, his hard breathing and his clenched teeth, showed that he was suffering beyond endurance. Near his right hand in a pool of blood lay a revolver.

"Don't go away," I heard a faint voice when the match had gone out. "There's a candle on the table."

I lighted the candle and stood still in the middle of the room not knowing what to do next. I stood and looked at the man on the floor, and it seemed to me that I had seen him before.

"The pain is insufferable," he whispered, "and I haven't the strength to shoot myself again. Incomprehensible lack of will."

I flung off my overcoat and attended to the sick man. Lifting him from the floor like a baby, I laid him on the American-leather covered sofa and carefully undressed him. He was shivering and cold when I took off his clothes; the wound which I saw was not in keeping either with his shivering nor the expression on his face. It was a trifling one. The bullet had passed between the fifth and sixth ribs on the left side, only piercing the skin and the flesh. I found the bullet itself in the folds of the coat-lining near the back pocket. Stopping the bleeding as best I could and making a temporary bandage of a pillow-case, a towel, and two handkerchiefs, I gave the wounded man some water and covered

ANTON CHEKHOV

him with a fur coat that was hanging in the passage. We neither of us said a word while the bandaging was being done. I did my work while he lay motionless looking at me with his eyes screwed up as though he were ashamed of his unsuccessful shot and the trouble he was giving me.

"Now I must trouble you to lie still," I said, when I had finished the bandaging, "while I run to the chemist and get something."

"No need!" he muttered, clutching me by the sleeve and opening his eyes wide.

I read terror in his eyes. He was afraid of my going away.

"No need! Stay another five minutes. . . ten. If it doesn't disgust you, do stay, I entreat you."

As he begged me he was trembling and his teeth were chattering. I obeyed, and sat down on the edge of the sofa. Ten minutes passed in silence. I sat silent, looking about the room into which fate had brought me so unexpectedly. What poverty! This man who was the possessor of a handsome, effeminate face and a luxuriant well-tended beard, had surroundings which a humble working man would not have envied. A sofa with its American-leather torn and peeling, a humble greasy-looking chair, a table covered with a little of paper, and a wretched oleograph on the wall, that was all I saw. Damp, gloomy, and grey.

"What a wind!" said the sick man, without opening his eyes, "How it whistles!"

"Yes," I said. "I say, I fancy I know you. Didn't you take part in some private theatricals in General Luhatchev's villa last year?"

"What of it?" he asked, quickly opening his eyes.

A cloud seemed to pass over his face.

"I certainly saw you there. Isn't your name Vassilyev?"

"If it is, what of it? It makes it no better that you should know me."

"No, but I just asked you."

Vassilyev closed his eyes and, as though offended, turned his face to the back of the sofa.

"I don't understand your curiosity," he muttered. "You'll be asking me next what it was drove me to commit suicide!"

Before a minute had passed, he turned round towards me again, opened his eyes and said in a tearful voice:

"Excuse me for taking such a tone, but you'll admit I'm right! To ask a convict how he got into prison, or a suicide why he shot himself is not generous. . . and indelicate. To think of gratifying idle curiosity at the expense of another man's nerves!"

brings back a whiff of spring. . . And now! What a cruel change of scene! There is a subject for you! Only don't you go in for writing 'the diary of a suicide.' That's vulgar and conventional. You make something humorous of it."

"Again you are. . . posing," I said. "There's nothing humorous in your position."

"Nothing laughable? You say nothing laughable?" Vassilyev sat up, and tears glistened in his eyes. An expression of bitter distress came into his pale face. His chin quivered.

"You laugh at the deceit of cheating clerks and faithless wives," he said, "but no clerk, no faithless wife has cheated as my fate has cheated me! I have been deceived as no bank depositor, no duped husband has ever been deceived! Only realise what an absurd fool I have been made! Last year before your eyes I did not know what to do with myself for happiness. And now before your eyes. . ."

Vassilyev's head sank on the pillow and he laughed.

"Nothing more absurd and stupid than such a change could possibly be imagined. Chapter one: spring, love, honeymoon. . . honey, in fact; chapter two: looking for a job, the pawnshop, pallor, the chemist's shop, and. . . to-morrow's splashing through the mud to the graveyard."

He laughed again. I felt acutely uncomfortable and made up my mind to go.

"I tell you what," I said, "you lie down, and I will go to the chemist's."

He made no answer. I put on my great-coat and went out of his room. As I crossed the passage I glanced at the coffin and Madame Mimotih reading over it. I strained my eyes in vain, I could not recognise in the swarthy, yellow face Zina, the lively, pretty *ingénue* of Luhatchev's company.

"*Sic transit*," I thought.

With that I went out, not forgetting to take the revolver, and made my way to the chemist's. But I ought not to have gone away. When I came back from the chemist's, Vassilyev lay on the sofa fainting. The bandages had been roughly torn off, and blood was flowing from the reopened wound. It was daylight before I succeeded in restoring him to consciousness. He was raving in delirium, shivering, and looking with unseeing eyes about the room till morning had come, and we heard the booming voice of the priest as he read the service over the dead.

When Vassilyev's rooms were crowded with old women and mutes, when the coffin had been moved and carried out of the yard, I advised him to remain at home. But he would not obey me, in spite of the pain and the grey, rainy morning. He walked bareheaded and in silence behind the coffin all the way to the cemetery, hardly able to move one leg after the other, and from time to time clutching convulsively at his wounded side. His face expressed complete apathy. Only once when I roused him from his lethargy by some insignificant question he shifted his eyes over the pavement and the grey fence, and for a moment there was a gleam of gloomy anger in them.

"'Weelright,'" he read on a signboard. "Ignorant, illiterate people, devil take them!"

I led him home from the cemetery.

ONLY ONE YEAR HAS PASSED since that night, and Vassilyev has hardly had time to wear out the boots in which he tramped through the mud behind his wife's coffin.

At the present time as I finish this story, he is sitting in my drawing-room and, playing on the piano, is showing the ladies how provincial misses sing sentimental songs. The ladies are laughing, and he is laughing too. He is enjoying himself.

I call him into my study. Evidently not pleased at my taking him from agreeable company, he comes to me and stands before me in the attitude of a man who has no time to spare. I give him this story, and ask him to read it. Always condescending about my authorship, he stifles a sigh, the sigh of a lazy reader, sits down in an armchair and begins upon it.

"Hang it all, what horrors," he mutters with a smile.

But the further he gets into the reading, the graver his face becomes. At last, under the stress of painful memories, he turns terribly pale, he gets up and goes on reading as he stands. When he has finished he begins pacing from corner to corner.

"How does it end?" I ask him.

"How does it end? H'm. . ."

He looks at the room, at me, at himself. . . He sees his new fashionable suit, hears the ladies laughing and. . . sinking on a chair, begins laughing as he laughed on that night.

"Wasn't I right when I told you it was all absurd? My God! I have had burdens to bear that would have broken an elephant's back; the devil knows what I have suffered—no one could have suffered more, I think, and where are the traces? It's astonishing. One would have thought the imprint made on a man by his agonies would have been everlasting, never to be effaced or eradicated. And yet that imprint wears out as easily as a pair of cheap boots. There is nothing left, not a scrap. It's as though I hadn't been suffering then, but had been dancing a mazurka. Everything in the world is transitory, and that transitoriness is absurd! A wide field for humorists! Tack on a humorous end, my friend!"

"Pyotr Nikolaevitch, are you coming soon?" The impatient ladies call my hero.

"This minute," answers the "vain and fatuous" man, setting his tie straight. "It's absurd and pitiful, my friend, pitiful and absurd, but what's to be done? *Homo sum.* . . And I praise Mother Nature all the same for her transmutation of substances. If we retained an agonising memory of toothache and of all the terrors which every one of us has had to experience, if all that were everlasting, we poor mortals would have a bad time of it in this life."

I look at his smiling face and I remember the despair and the horror with which his eyes were filled a year ago when he looked at the dark window. I see him, entering into his habitual rôle of intellectual chatterer, prepare to show off his idle theories, such as the transmutation of substances before me, and at the same time I recall him sitting on the floor in a pool of blood with his sick imploring eyes.

"How will it end?" I ask myself aloud.

Vassilyev, whistling and straightening his tie, walks off into the drawing-room, and I look after him, and feel vexed. For some reason I regret his past sufferings, I regret all that I felt myself on that man's account on that terrible night. It is as though I had lost something. . .

Mari D'Elle

It was a free night. Natalya Andreyevna Bronin (her married name was Nikitin), the opera singer, is lying in her bedroom, her whole being abandoned to repose. She lies, deliciously drowsy, thinking of her little daughter who lives somewhere far away with her grandmother or aunt. . . The child is more precious to her than the public, bouquets, notices in the papers, adorers. . . and she would be glad to think about her till morning. She is happy, at peace, and all she longs for is not to be prevented from lying undisturbed, dozing and dreaming of her little girl.

All at once the singer starts, and opens her eyes wide: there is a harsh abrupt ring in the entry. Before ten seconds have passed the bell tinkles a second time and a third time. The door is opened noisily and some one walks into the entry stamping his feet like a horse, snorting and puffing with the cold.

"Damn it all, nowhere to hang one's coat!" the singer hears a husky bass voice. "Celebrated singer, look at that! Makes five thousand a year, and can't get a decent hat-stand!"

"My husband!" thinks the singer, frowning. "And I believe he has brought one of his friends to stay the night too. . . Hateful!"

No more peace. When the loud noise of some one blowing his nose and putting off his goloshes dies away, the singer hears cautious footsteps in her bedroom. . . It is her husband, *mari d'elle*, Denis Petrovitch Nikitin. He brings a whiff of cold air and a smell of brandy. For a long while he walks about the bedroom, breathing heavily, and, stumbling against the chairs in the dark, seems to be looking for something. . .

"What do you want?" his wife moans, when she is sick of his fussing about. "You have woken me."

"I am looking for the matches, my love. You. . . you are not asleep then? I have brought you a message. . . Greetings from that. . . what's-his-name? . . . red-headed fellow who is always sending you bouquets. . . Zagvozdkin. . . I have just been to see him."

"What did you go to him for?"

"Oh, nothing particular. . . We sat and talked and had a drink. Say what you like, Nathalie, I dislike that individual—I dislike him awfully! He is a rare blockhead. He is a wealthy man, a capitalist; he has six hundred thousand, and you would never guess it. Money is no more use to him than a radish to a dog. He does not eat it himself nor give it to others. Money ought to circulate, but he keeps tight hold of it, is afraid to part with it. . . What's the good of capital lying idle? Capital lying idle is no better than grass."

Mari d'elle gropes his way to the edge of the bed and, puffing, sits down at his wife's feet.

"Capital lying idle is pernicious," he goes on. "Why has business gone downhill in Russia? Because there is so much capital lying idle among us; they are afraid to invest it. It's very different in England. . . There are no such queer fish as Zagvozdkin in England, my girl. . . There every farthing is in circulation. . . Yes. . . They don't keep it locked up in chests there. . ."

"Well, that's all right. I am sleepy."

"Directly. . . Whatever was it I was talking about? Yes. . . In these hard times hanging is too good for Zagvozdkin. . . He is a fool and a scoundrel. . . No better than a fool. If I asked him for a loan without security—why, a child could see that he runs no risk whatever. He doesn't understand, the ass! For ten thousand he would have got a hundred. In a year he would have another hundred thousand. I asked, I talked. . . but he wouldn't give it me, the blockhead."

"I hope you did not ask him for a loan in my name."

"H'm. . . A queer question. . ." *Mari d'elle* is offended. "Anyway he would sooner give me ten thousand than you. You are a woman, and I am a man anyway, a business-like person. And what a scheme I propose to him! Not a bubble, not some chimera, but a sound thing, substantial! If one could hit on a man who would understand, one might get twenty thousand for the idea alone! Even you would understand if I were to tell you about it. Only you. . . don't chatter about it. . . not a word. . . but I fancy I have talked to you about it already. Have I talked to you about sausage-skins?"

"M'm. . . by and by."

"I believe I have. . . Do you see the point of it? Now the provision shops and the sausage-makers get their sausage-skins locally, and pay a high price for them. Well, but if one were to bring sausage-skins from the Caucasus where they are worth nothing, and where they are thrown away, then. . . where do you suppose the sausage-makers would buy their skins, here in the slaughterhouses or from me? From me, of course! Why, I shall sell them ten times as cheap! Now let us look at it like this: every year in Petersburg and Moscow and in other centres these same skins would be bought to the. . . to the sum of five hundred thousand, let us suppose. That's the minimum. Well, and if. . ."

"You can tell me to-morrow. . . later on. . ."

"Yes, that's true. You are sleepy, *pardon*, I am just going. . . say what you like, but with capital you can do good business everywhere, wherever you go. . . With capital even out of cigarette ends one may make a million. . . Take your theatrical business now. Why, for example, did Lentovsky come to grief? It's very simple. He did not go the right way to work from the very first. He had no capital and he went headlong to the dogs. . . He ought first to have secured his capital, and then to have gone slowly and cautiously. . . Nowadays, one can easily make money by a theatre, whether it is a private one or a people's one. . . If one produces the right plays, charges a low price for admission, and hits the public fancy, one may put a hundred thousand in one's pocket the first year. . . You don't understand, but I am talking sense. . . You see you are fond of hoarding capital; you are no better than that fool Zagvozdkin, you heap it up and don't know what for. . . You won't listen, you don't want to. . . If you were to put it into circulation, you wouldn't have to be rushing all over the place. . . You see for a private theatre, five thousand would be enough for a beginning. . . Not like Lentovsky, of course, but on a modest scale in a small way. I have got a manager already, I have looked at a suitable building. . . It's only the money I haven't got. . . If only you understood things you would have parted with your Five per cents. . . your Preference shares. . ."

"No, *merci*. . . You have fleeced me enough already. . . Let me alone, I have been punished already. . ."

"If you are going to argue like a woman, then of course. . ." sighs Nikitin, getting up. "Of course. . ."

"Let me alone. . . Come, go away and don't keep me awake. . . I am sick of listening to your nonsense."

"H'm. . . To be sure. . . of course! Fleeced. . . plundered. . . What we give we remember, but we don't remember what we take."

"I have never taken anything from you."

"Is that so? But when we weren't a celebrated singer, at whose expense did we live then? And who, allow me to ask, lifted you out of beggary and secured your happiness? Don't you remember that?"

"Come, go to bed. Go along and sleep it off."

"Do you mean to say you think I am drunk? . . . if I am so low in the eyes of such a grand lady. . . I can go away altogether."

"Do. A good thing too."

"I will, too. I have humbled myself enough. And I will go."

"Oh, my God! Oh, do go, then! I shall be delighted!"

"Very well, we shall see."

Nikitin mutters something to himself, and, stumbling over the chairs, goes out of the bedroom. Then sounds reach her from the entry of whispering, the shuffling of goloshes and a door being shut. *Mari d'elle* has taken offence in earnest and gone out.

"Thank God, he has gone!" thinks the singer. "Now I can sleep."

And as she falls asleep she thinks of her *mari d'elle*, what sort of a man he is, and how this affliction has come upon her. At one time he used to live at Tchernigov, and had a situation there as a book-keeper. As an ordinary obscure individual and not the *mari d'elle*, he had been quite endurable: he used to go to his work and take his salary, and all his whims and projects went no further than a new guitar, fashionable trousers, and an amber cigarette-holder. Since he had become "the husband of a celebrity" he was completely transformed. The singer remembered that when first she told him she was going on the stage he had made a fuss, been indignant, complained to her parents, turned her out of the house. She had been obliged to go on the stage without his permission. Afterwards, when he learned from the papers and from various people that she was earning big sums, he had 'forgiven her,' abandoned book-keeping, and become her hanger-on. The singer was overcome with amazement when she looked at her hanger-on: when and where had he managed to pick up new tastes, polish, and airs and graces? Where had he learned the taste of oysters and of different Burgundies? Who had taught him to dress and do his hair in the fashion and call her 'Nathalie' instead of Natasha?"

"It's strange," thinks the singer. "In old days he used to get his salary and put it away, but now a hundred roubles a day is not enough for him. In old days he was afraid to talk before schoolboys for fear of saying something silly, and now he is overfamiliar even with princes. . . wretched, contemptible little creature!"

But then the singer starts again; again there is the clang of the bell in the entry. The housemaid, scolding and angrily flopping with her slippers, goes to open the door. Again some one comes in and stamps like a horse.

"He has come back!" thinks the singer. "When shall I be left in peace? It's revolting!" She is overcome by fury.

"Wait a bit. . . I'll teach you to get up these farces! You shall go away. I'll make you go away!"

The singer leaps up and runs barefoot into the little drawing-room where her *mari* usually sleeps. She comes at the moment when he is undressing, and carefully folding his clothes on a chair.

"You went away!" she says, looking at him with bright eyes full of hatred. "What did you come back for?"

Nikitin remains silent, and merely sniffs.

"You went away! Kindly take yourself off this very minute! This very minute! Do you hear?"

Mari d'elle coughs and, without looking at his wife, takes off his braces.

"If you don't go away, you insolent creature, I shall go," the singer goes on, stamping her bare foot, and looking at him with flashing eyes. "I shall go! Do you hear, insolent. . . worthless wretch, flunkey, out you go!"

"You might have some shame before outsiders," mutters her husband. . .

The singer looks round and only then sees an unfamiliar countenance that looks like an actor's. . . The countenance, seeing the singer's uncovered shoulders and bare feet, shows signs of embarrassment, and looks ready to sink through the floor.

"Let me introduce. . ." mutters Nikitin, "Bezbozhnikov, a provincial manager."

The singer utters a shriek, and runs off into her bedroom.

"There, you see. . ." says *mari d'elle*, as he stretches himself on the sofa, "it was all honey just now. . . my love, my dear, my darling, kisses and embraces. . . but as soon as money is touched upon, then. . . As you see. . . money is the great thing. . . Good night!"

A minute later there is a snore.

A LIVING CHATTEL

I

GROHOLSKY EMBRACED LIZA, KEPT KISSING one after another all
her little fingers with their bitten pink nails, and laid her on the couch
covered with cheap velvet. Liza crossed one foot over the other, clasped
her hands behind her head, and lay down.

Groholsky sat down in a chair beside her and bent over. He was
entirely absorbed in contemplation of her.

How pretty she seemed to him, lighted up by the rays of the setting
sun!

There was a complete view from the window of the setting sun,
golden, lightly flecked with purple.

The whole drawing-room, including Liza, was bathed by it with
brilliant light that did not hurt the eyes, and for a little while covered
with gold.

Groholsky was lost in admiration. Liza was so incredibly beautiful.
It is true her little kittenish face with its brown eyes, and turn up nose
was fresh, and even piquant, his scanty hair was black as soot and curly,
her little figure was graceful, well proportioned and mobile as the body
of an electric eel, but on the whole. . . However my taste has nothing
to do with it. Groholsky who was spoilt by women, and who had been
in love and out of love hundreds of times in his life, saw her as a beauty.
He loved her, and blind love finds ideal beauty everywhere.

"I say," he said, looking straight into her eyes, "I have come to talk
to you, my precious. Love cannot bear anything vague or indefinite. . .
Indefinite relations, you know, I told you yesterday, Liza. . . we will try
to-day to settle the question we raised yesterday. Come, let us decide
together. . ."

"What are we to do?"

Liza gave a yawn and scowling, drew her right arm from under her
head.

"What are we to do?" she repeated hardly audibly after Groholsky.

"Well, yes, what are we to do? Come, decide, wise little head. . . I
love you, and a man in love is not fond of sharing. He is more than an
egoist. It is too much for me to go shares with your husband. I mentally
tear him to pieces, when I remember that he loves you too. In the

second place you love me. . . Perfect freedom is an essential condition for love. . . And are you free? Are you not tortured by the thought that that man towers for ever over your soul? A man whom you do not love, whom very likely and quite naturally, you hate. . . That's the second thing. . . And thirdly. . . What is the third thing? Oh yes. . . We are deceiving him and that. . . is dishonourable. Truth before everything, Liza. Let us have done with lying!"

"Well, then, what are we to do?"

"You can guess. . . I think it necessary, obligatory, to inform him of our relations and to leave him, to begin to live in freedom. Both must be done as quickly as possible. . . This very evening, for instance. . . It's time to make an end of it. Surely you must be sick of loving like a thief?"

"Tell! tell Vanya?"

"Why, yes!"

"That's impossible! I told you yesterday, Michel, that it is impossible."

"Why?"

"He will be upset. He'll make a row, do all sorts of unpleasant things. . . Don't you know what he is like? God forbid! There's no need to tell him. What an idea!"

Groholsky passed his hand over his brow, and heaved a sigh.

"Yes," he said, "he will be more than upset. I am robbing him of his happiness. Does he love you?"

"He does love me. Very much."

"There's another complication! One does not know where to begin. To conceal it from him is base, telling him would kill him. . . Goodness knows what's one to do. Well, how is it to be?"

Groholsky pondered. His pale face wore a frown.

"Let us go on always as we are now," said Liza. "Let him find out for himself, if he wants to."

"But you know that. . . is sinful, and besides the fact is you are mine, and no one has the right to think that you do not belong to me but to someone else! You are mine! I will not give way to anyone! . . . I am sorry for him—God knows how sorry I am for him, Liza! It hurts me to see him! But. . . it can't be helped after all. You don't love him, do you? What's the good of your going on being miserable with him? We must have it out! We will have it out with him, and you will come to me. You are my wife, and not his. Let him do what he likes. He'll get over his troubles somehow. . . He is not the first, and he won't be the last. . . Will you run away? Eh? Make haste and tell me! Will you run away?"

Liza got up and looked inquiringly at Groholsky.

"Run away?"

"Yes. . . To my estate. . . Then to the Crimea. . . We will tell him by letter. . . We can go at night. There is a train at half past one. Well? Is that all right?"

Liza scratched the bridge of her nose, and hesitated.

"Very well," she said, and burst into tears.

Patches of red came out of her cheeks, her eyes swelled, and tears flowed down her kittenish face. . .

"What is it?" cried Groholsky in a flutter. "Liza! what's the matter? Come! what are you crying for? What a girl! Come, what is it? Darling! Little woman!"

Liza held out her hands to Groholsky, and hung on his neck. There was a sound of sobbing.

"I am sorry for him. . ." muttered Liza. "Oh, I am so sorry for him!"

"Sorry for whom?"

"Va—Vanya. . ."

"And do you suppose I'm not? But what's to be done? We are causing him suffering. . . He will be unhappy, will curse us. . . but is it our fault that we love one another?"

As he uttered the last word, Groholsky darted away from Liza as though he had been stung and sat down in an easy chair. Liza sprang away from his neck and rapidly—in one instant—dropped on the lounge.

They both turned fearfully red, dropped their eyes, and coughed.

A tall, broad-shouldered man of thirty, in the uniform of a government clerk, had walked into the drawing-room. He had walked in unnoticed. Only the bang of a chair which he knocked in the doorway had warned the lovers of his presence, and made them look round. It was the husband.

They had looked round too late.

He had seen Groholsky's arm round Liza's waist, and had seen Liza hanging on Groholsky's white and aristocratic neck.

"He saw us!" Liza and Groholsky thought at the same moment, while they did not know what to do with their heavy hands and embarrassed eyes. . .

The petrified husband, rosy-faced, turned white.

An agonising, strange, soul-revolting silence lasted for three minutes. Oh, those three minutes! Groholsky remembers them to this day.

The first to move and break the silence was the husband. He stepped up to Groholsky and, screwing his face into a senseless grimace like a smile, gave him his hand. Groholsky shook the soft perspiring hand and shuddered all over as though he had crushed a cold frog in his fist.

"Good evening," he muttered.

"How are you?" the husband brought out in a faint husky, almost inaudible voice, and he sat down opposite Groholsky, straightening his collar at the back of his neck.

Again, an agonising silence followed. . . but that silence was no longer so stupid. . . The first step, most difficult and colourless, was over.

All that was left now was for one of the two to depart in search of matches or on some such trifling errand. Both longed intensely to get away. They sat still, not looking at one another, and pulled at their beards while they ransacked their troubled brains for some means of escape from their horribly awkward position. Both were perspiring. Both were unbearably miserable and both were devoured by hatred. They longed to begin the tussle but how were they to begin and which was to begin first? If only she would have gone out!

"I saw you yesterday at the Assembly Hall," muttered Bugrov (that was the husband's name).

"Yes, I was there. . . the ball. . . did you dance?"

"M'm. . . yes. . . with that. . . with the younger Lyukovtsky. . . She dances heavily. . . She dances impossibly. She is a great chatterbox." (Pause.) "She is never tired of talking."

"Yes. . . It was slow. I saw you too. . ."

Groholsky accidentally glanced at Bugrov. . . He caught the shifting eyes of the deceived husband and could not bear it. He got up quickly, quickly seized Bugrov's hand, shook it, picked up his hat, and walked towards the door, conscious of his own back. He felt as though thousands of eyes were looking at his back. It is a feeling known to the actor who has been hissed and is making his exit from the stage, and to the young dandy who has received a blow on the back of the head and is being led away in charge of a policeman.

As soon as the sound of Groholsky's steps had died away and the door in the hall creaked, Bugrov leapt up, and after making two or three rounds of the drawing-room, strolled up to his wife. The kittenish face puckered up and began blinking its eyes as though expecting a slap. Her husband went up to her, and with a pale, distorted face, with arms, head, and shoulders shaking, stepped on her dress and knocked her knees with his.

"If, you wretched creature," he began in a hollow, wailing voice, "you let him come here once again, I'll. . . Don't let him dare to set his foot. . . I'll kill you. Do you understand? A-a-ah. . . worthless creature, you shudder! Fil-thy woman!"

Bugrov seized her by the elbow, shook her, and flung her like an indiarubber ball towards the window. . .

"Wretched, vulgar woman! you have no shame!"

She flew towards the window, hardly touching the floor with her feet, and caught at the curtains with her hands.

"Hold your tongue," shouted her husband, going up to her with flashing eyes and stamping his foot.

She did hold her tongue, she looked at the ceiling, and whimpered while her face wore the expression of a little girl in disgrace expecting to be punished.

"So that's what you are like! Eh? Carrying on with a fop! Good! And your promise before the altar? What are you? A nice wife and mother. Hold your tongue!"

And he struck her on her pretty supple shoulder. "Hold your tongue, you wretched creature. I'll give you worse than that! If that scoundrel dares to show himself here ever again, if I see you—listen!—with that blackguard ever again, don't ask for mercy! I'll kill you, if I go to Siberia for it! And him too. I shouldn't think twice about it! You can go, I don't want to see you!"

Bugrov wiped his eyes and his brow with his sleeve and strode about the drawing-room, Liza sobbing more and more loudly, twitching her shoulders and her little turned up nose, became absorbed in examining the lace on the curtain.

"You are crazy," her husband shouted. "Your silly head is full of nonsense! Nothing but whims! I won't allow it, Elizaveta, my girl! You had better be careful with me! I don't like it! If you want to behave like a pig, then. . . then out you go, there is no place in my house for you! Out you pack if. . . You are a wife, so you must forget these dandies, put them out of your silly head! It's all foolishness! Don't let it happen again! You try defending yourself! Love your husband! You have been given to your husband, so you must love him. Yes, indeed! Is one not enough? Go away till. . . Torturers!"

Bugrov paused; then shouted:

"Go away I tell you, go to the nursery! Why are you blubbering, it is your own fault, and you blubber! What a woman! Last year you were after Petka Totchkov, now you are after this devil. Lord forgive us! . . . Tfoo, it's time you understood what you are! A wife! A mother! Last year there were unpleasantnesses, and now there will be unpleasantnesses. . . Tfoo!"

Bugrov heaved a loud sigh, and the air was filled with the smell of sherry. He had come back from dining and was slightly drunk. . .

"Don't you know your duty? No! . . . you must be taught, you've not been taught so far! Your mamma was a gad-about, and you. . . you can blubber. Yes! blubber away. . ."

Bugrov went up to his wife and drew the curtain out of her hands.

"Don't stand by the window, people will see you blubbering. . . Don't let it happen again. You'll go from embracing to worse trouble. You'll come to grief. Do you suppose I like to be made a fool of? And you will make a fool of me if you carry on with them, the low brutes. . . Come, that's enough. . . Don't you. . . Another time. . . Of course I . . Liza. . . stay. . ."

Bugrov heaved a sigh and enveloped Liza in the fumes of sherry.

"You are young and silly, you don't understand anything. . . I am never at home. . . And they take advantage of it. You must be sensible, prudent. They will deceive you. And then I won't endure it. . . Then I may do anything. . . Of course! Then you can just lie down, and die. I. . . I am capable of doing anything if you deceive me, my good girl. I might beat you to death. . . And. . . I shall turn you out of the house, and then you can go to your rascals."

And Bugrov (*horribile dictu*) wiped the wet, tearful face of the traitress Liza with his big soft hand. He treated his twenty-year-old wife as though she were a child.

"Come, that's enough. . . I forgive you. Only God forbid it should happen again! I forgive you for the fifth time, but I shall not forgive you for the sixth, as God is holy. God does not forgive such as you for such things."

Bugrov bent down and put out his shining lips towards Liza's little head. But the kiss did not follow. The doors of the hall, of the dining-room, of the parlour, and of the drawing-room all slammed, and Groholsky flew into the drawing-room like a whirlwind. He was pale and trembling. He was flourishing his arms and crushing his expensive hat in his hands. His coat fluttered upon him as though it were on a peg. He was the incarnation of acute fever. When Bugrov saw him he moved away from his wife and began looking out of the other window. Groholsky flew up to him, and waving his arms and breathing heavily and looking at no one, he began in a shaking voice:

"Ivan Petrovitch! Let us leave off keeping up this farce with one another! We have deceived each other long enough! It's too much! I cannot stand it. You must do as you like, but I cannot! It's hateful and mean, it's revolting! Do you understand that it is revolting?"

Groholsky spluttered and gasped for breath.

"It's against my principles. And you are an honest man. I love her! I love her more than anything on earth! You have noticed it and. . . it's my duty to say this!"

"What am I to say to him?" Ivan Petrovitch wondered.

"We must make an end of it. This farce cannot drag on much longer! It must be settled somehow."

Groholsky drew a breath and went on:

"I cannot live without her; she feels the same. You are an educated man, you will understand that in such circumstances your family life is impossible. This woman is not yours, so. . . in short, I beg you to look at the matter from an indulgent humane point of view. . . Ivan Petrovitch, you must understand at last that I love her—love her more than myself, more than anything in the world, and to struggle against that love is beyond my power!"

"And she?" Bugrov asked in a sullen, somewhat ironical tone.

"Ask her; come now, ask her! For her to live with a man she does not love, to live with you is. . . is a misery!"

"And she?" Bugrov repeated, this time not in an ironical tone.

"She. . . she loves me! We love each other, Ivan Petrovitch! Kill us, despise us, pursue us, do as you will, but we can no longer conceal it from you. We are standing face to face—you may judge us with all the severity of a man whom we. . . whom fate has robbed of happiness!"

Bugrov turned as red as a boiled crab, and looked out of one eye at Liza. He began blinking. His fingers, his lips, and his eyelids twitched. Poor fellow! The eyes of his weeping wife told him that Groholsky was right, that it was a serious matter.

"Well!" he muttered. "If you. . . In these days. . . You are always. . ."

"As God is above," Groholsky shrilled in his high tenor, "we understand you. Do you suppose we have no sense, no feeling? I know what agonies I am causing you, as God's above! But be indulgent, I beseech you! We are not to blame. Love is not a crime. No will can struggle against it. . . Give her up to me, Ivan Petrovitch! Let her go with me! Take from me what you will for your sufferings. Take my life, but give me Liza. I am ready to do anything. . . Come, tell me how I can do something to make up in part at least! To make up for that lost happiness, I can give you other happiness. I can, Ivan Petrovitch; I am ready to do anything! It would be base on my part to leave you without satisfaction. . . I understand you at this moment."

Bugrov waved his hand as though to say, 'For God's sake, go away.' His eyes began to be dimmed by a treacherous moisture—in a moment they would see him crying like a child.

"I understand you, Ivan Petrovitch. I will give you another happiness, such as hitherto you have not known. What would you like? I have money, my father is an influential man. . . Will you? Come, how much do you want?"

Bugrov's heart suddenly began throbbing. . . He clutched at the window curtains with both hands. . .

"Will you have fifty thousand? Ivan Petrovitch, I entreat you. . . It's not a bribe, not a bargain. . . I only want by a sacrifice on my part to atone a little for your inevitable loss. Would you like a hundred thousand? I am willing. A hundred thousand?"

My God! Two immense hammers began beating on the perspiring temples of the unhappy Ivan Petrovitch. Russian sledges with tinkling bells began racing in his ears. . .

"Accept this sacrifice from me," Groholsky went on, "I entreat you! You will take a load off my conscience. . . I implore you!"

My God! A smart carriage rolled along the road wet from a May shower, passed the window through which Bugrov's wet eyes were looking. The horses were fine, spirited, well-trained beasts. People in straw hats, with contented faces, were sitting in the carriage with long fishing-rods and bags. . . A schoolboy in a white cap was holding a gun. They were driving out into the country to catch fish, to shoot, to walk about and have tea in the open air. They were driving to that region of bliss in which Bugrov as a boy—the barefoot, sunburnt, but infinitely happy son of a village deacon—had once raced about the meadows, the woods, and the river banks. Oh, how fiendishly seductive was that May! How happy those who can take off their heavy uniforms, get into a carriage and fly off to the country where the quails are calling and there is the scent of fresh hay. Bugrov's heart ached with a sweet thrill that made him shiver. A hundred thousand! With the carriage there floated before him all the secret dreams over which he had gloated, through the long years of his life as a government clerk as he sat in the office of his department or in his wretched little study. . . A river, deep, with fish, a wide garden with narrow avenues, little fountains, shade, flowers, arbours, a luxurious villa with terraces and turrets with an Aeolian harp and little silver bells (he had heard of the existence of an Aeolian harp from German romances); a cloudless blue sky; pure limpid air fragrant with the scents that recall his hungry, barefoot, crushed childhood. . . To get up at five, to go to bed at nine; to spend the day catching fish, talking with the peasants. . . What happiness!

"Ivan Petrovitch, do not torture me! Will you take a hundred thousand?"

"H'm. . . a hundred and fifty thousand!" muttered Bugrov in a hollow voice, the voice of a husky bull. He muttered it, and bowed his head, ashamed of his words, and awaiting the answer.

"Good," said Groholsky, "I agree. I thank you, Ivan Petrovitch. . . In a minute. . . I will not keep you waiting. . ."

Groholsky jumped up, put on his hat, and staggering backwards, ran out of the drawing-room.

Bugrov clutched the window curtains more tightly than ever. . . He was ashamed. . . There was a nasty, stupid feeling in his soul, but, on the other hand, what fair shining hopes swarmed between his throbbing temples! He was rich!

Liza, who had grasped nothing of what was happening, darted through the half-opened door trembling all over and afraid that he would come to her window and fling her away from it. She went into the nursery, laid herself down on the nurse's bed, and curled herself up. She was shivering with fever.

Bugrov was left alone. He felt stifled, and he opened the window. What glorious air breathed fragrance on his face and neck! It would be good to breathe such air lolling on the cushions of a carriage. . . Out there, far beyond the town, among the villages and the summer villas, the air was sweeter still. . . Bugrov actually smiled as he dreamed of the air that would be about him when he would go out on the verandah of his villa and admire the view. A long while he dreamed. . . The sun had set, and still he stood and dreamed, trying his utmost to cast out of his mind the image of Liza which obstinately pursued him in all his dreams.

"I have brought it, Ivan Petrovitch!" Groholsky, re-entering, whispered above his ear. "I have brought it—take it. . . Here in this roll there are forty thousand. . . With this cheque will you kindly get twenty the day after to-morrow from Valentinov? . . . Here is a bill of exchange. . . a cheque. . . The remaining thirty thousand in a day or two. . . My steward will bring it to you."

Groholsky, pink and excited, with all his limbs in motion, laid before Bugrov a heap of rolls of notes and bundles of papers. The heap was big, and of all sorts of hues and tints. Never in the course of his life had Bugrov seen such a heap. He spread out his fat fingers and, not looking at Groholsky, fell to going through the bundles of notes and bonds. . .

Groholsky spread out all the money, and moved restlessly about the room, looking for the Dulcinea who had been bought and sold.

Filling his pockets and his pocket-book, Bugrov thrust the securities into the table drawer, and, drinking off half a decanter full of water, dashed out into the street.

"Cab!" he shouted in a frantic voice.

At half-past eleven that night he drove up to the entrance of the Paris Hotel. He went noisily upstairs and knocked at the door of Groholsky's apartments. He was admitted. Groholsky was packing his things in a portmanteau, Liza was sitting at the table trying on bracelets. They were both frightened when Bugrov went in to them. They fancied that he had come for Liza and had brought back the money which he had taken in haste without reflection. But Bugrov had not come for Liza. Ashamed of his new get-up and feeling frightfully awkward in it, he bowed and stood at the door in the attitude of a flunkey. The get-up was superb. Bugrov was unrecognisable. His huge person, which had never hitherto worn anything but a uniform, was clothed in a fresh, brand-new suit of fine French cloth and of the most fashionable cut. On his feet spats shone with sparkling buckles. He stood ashamed of his new get-up, and with his right hand covered the watch-chain for which he had, an hour before, paid three hundred roubles.

"I have come about something," he began. "A business agreement is beyond price. I am not going to give up Mishutka. . ."

"What Mishutka?" asked Groholsky.

"My son."

Groholsky and Liza looked at each other. Liza's eyes bulged, her cheeks flushed, and her lips twitched. . .

"Very well," she said.

She thought of Mishutka's warm little cot. It would be cruel to exchange that warm little cot for a chilly sofa in the hotel, and she consented.

"I shall see him," she said.

Bugrov bowed, walked out, and flew down the stairs in his splendour, cleaving the air with his expensive cane. . .

"Home," he said to the cabman. "I am starting at five o'clock to-morrow morning. . . You will come; if I am asleep, you will wake me. We are driving out of town."

II

IT WAS A LOVELY AUGUST evening. The sun, set in a golden background lightly flecked with purple, stood above the western horizon on the point of sinking behind the far-away tumuli. In the garden, shadows and half-shadows had vanished, and the air had grown damp, but the golden light was still playing on the tree-tops. . . It was warm. . . Rain had just fallen, and made the fresh, transparent fragrant air still fresher.

I am not describing the August of Petersburg or Moscow, foggy, tearful, and dark, with its cold, incredibly damp sunsets. God forbid! I am not describing our cruel northern August. I ask the reader to move with me to the Crimea, to one of its shores, not far from Feodosia, the spot where stands the villa of one of our heroes. It is a pretty, neat villa surrounded by flower-beds and clipped bushes. A hundred paces behind it is an orchard in which its inmates walk. . . Groholsky pays a high rent for that villa, a thousand roubles a year, I believe. . . The villa is not worth that rent, but it is pretty. . . Tall, with delicate walls and very delicate parapets, fragile, slender, painted a pale blue colour, hung with curtains, *portières*, draperies, it suggests a charming, fragile Chinese lady. . .

On the evening described above, Groholsky and Liza were sitting on the verandah of this villa. Groholsky was reading *Novoye Vremya* and drinking milk out of a green mug. A syphon of Seltzer water was standing on the table before him. Groholsky imagined that he was suffering from catarrh of the lungs, and by the advice of Dr. Dmitriev consumed an immense quantity of grapes, milk, and Seltzer water. Liza was sitting in a soft easy chair some distance from the table. With her elbows on the parapet, and her little face propped on her little fists, she was gazing at the villa opposite. . . The sun was playing upon the windows of the villa opposite, the glittering panes reflected the dazzling light. . . Beyond the little garden and the few trees that surrounded the villa there was a glimpse of the sea with its waves, its dark blue colour, its immensity, its white masts. . . It was so delightful! Groholsky was reading an article by Anonymous, and after every dozen lines he raised his blue eyes to Liza's back. . . The same passionate, fervent love was shining in those eyes still. . . He was infinitely happy in spite of his imaginary catarrh of the lungs. . . Liza was conscious of his eyes upon her back, and was thinking of Mishutka's brilliant future, and she felt so comfortable, so serene. . .

She was not so much interested by the sea, and the glittering reflection on the windows of the villa opposite as by the waggons which were trailing up to that villa one after another.

The waggons were full of furniture and all sorts of domestic articles. Liza watched the trellis gates and big glass doors of the villa being opened and the men bustling about the furniture and wrangling incessantly. Big armchairs and a sofa covered with dark raspberry coloured velvet, tables for the hall, the drawing-room and the dining-room, a big double bed and a child's cot were carried in by the glass doors; something big, wrapped up in sacking, was carried in too. A grand piano, thought Liza, and her heart throbbed.

It was long since she had heard the piano, and she was so fond of it. They had not a single musical instrument in their villa. Groholsky and she were musicians only in soul, no more. There were a great many boxes and packages with the words: "with care" upon them carried in after the piano.

They were boxes of looking-glasses and crockery. A gorgeous and luxurious carriage was dragged in, at the gate, and two white horses were led in looking like swans.

"My goodness, what riches!" thought Liza, remembering her old pony which Groholsky, who did not care for riding, had bought her for a hundred roubles. Compared with those swan-like steeds, her pony seemed to her no better than a bug. Groholsky, who was afraid of riding fast, had purposely bought Liza a poor horse.

"What wealth!" Liza thought and murmured as she gazed at the noisy carriers.

The sun hid behind the tumuli, the air began to lose its dryness and limpidity, and still the furniture was being driven up and hauled into the house. At last it was so dark that Groholsky left off reading the newspaper while Liza still gazed and gazed.

"Shouldn't we light the lamp?" said Groholsky, afraid that a fly might drop into his milk and be swallowed in the darkness.

"Liza! shouldn't we light the lamp? Shall we sit in darkness, my angel?"

Liza did not answer. She was interested in a chaise which had driven up to the villa opposite. . . What a charming little mare was in that chaise. Of medium size, not large, but graceful. . . A gentleman in a top hat was sitting in the chaise, a child about three, apparently a boy, was sitting on his knees waving his little hands. . . He was waving his little hands and shouting with delight.

Liza suddenly uttered a shriek, rose from her seat and lurched forward.

"What is the matter?" asked Groholsky.

"Nothing. . . I only. . . I fancied. . ."

The tall, broad-shouldered gentleman in the top hat jumped out of the chaise, lifted the boy down, and with a skip and a hop ran gaily in at the glass door. The door opened noisily and he vanished into the darkness of the villa apartments.

Two smart footmen ran up to the horse in the chaise, and most respectfully led it to the gate. Soon the villa opposite was lighted up, and the clatter of plates, knives, and forks was audible. The gentleman in the top hat was having his supper, and judging by the duration of the clatter of crockery, his supper lasted long. Liza fancied she could smell chicken soup and roast duck. After supper discordant sounds of the piano floated across from the villa. In all probability the gentleman in the top hat was trying to amuse the child in some way, and allowing it to strum on it.

Groholsky went up to Liza and put his arm round her waist.

"What wonderful weather!" he said. "What air! Do you feel it? I am very happy, Liza, very happy indeed. My happiness is so great that I am really afraid of its destruction. The greatest things are usually destroyed, and do you know, Liza, in spite of all my happiness, I am not absolutely. . . at peace. . . One haunting thought torments me. . . it torments me horribly. It gives me no peace by day or by night. . ."

"What thought?"

"An awful thought, my love. I am tortured by the thought of your husband. I have been silent hitherto. I have feared to trouble your inner peace, but I cannot go on being silent. Where is he? What has happened to him? What has become of him with his money? It is awful! Every night I see his face, exhausted, suffering, imploring. . . Why, only think, my angel—can the money he so generously accepted make up to him for you? He loved you very much, didn't he?"

"Very much!"

"There you see! He has either taken to drink now, or. . . I am anxious about him! Ah, how anxious I am! Should we write to him, do you think? We ought to comfort him. . . a kind word, you know."

Groholsky heaved a deep sigh, shook his head, and sank into an easy chair exhausted by painful reflection. Leaning his head on his fists he fell to musing. Judging from his face, his musings were painful.

"I am going to bed," said Liza; "it's time."

Liza went to her own room, undressed, and dived under the bedclothes. She used to go to bed at ten o'clock and get up at ten. She was fond of her comfort.

She was soon in the arms of Morpheus. Throughout the whole night she had the most fascinating dreams. . . She dreamed whole romances, novels, Arabian Nights. . . The hero of all these dreams was the gentleman in the top hat, who had caused her to utter a shriek that evening.

The gentleman in the top hat was carrying her off from Groholsky, was singing, was beating Groholsky and her, was flogging the boy under the window, was declaring his love, and driving her off in the chaise. . . Oh, dreams! In one night, lying with one's eyes shut, one may sometimes live through more than ten years of happiness. . . That night Liza lived through a great variety of experiences, and very happy ones, even in spite of the beating.

Waking up between six and seven, she flung on her clothes, hurriedly did her hair, and without even putting on her Tatar slippers with pointed toes, ran impulsively on to the verandah. Shading her eyes from the sun with one hand, and with the other holding up her slipping clothes, she gazed at the villa opposite. Her face beamed. . . There could be no further doubt it was he.

On the verandah in the villa opposite there was a table in front of the glass door. A tea service was shining and glistening on the table with a silver samovar at the head. Ivan Petrovitch was sitting at the table. He had in his hand a glass in a silver holder, and was drinking tea. He was drinking it with great relish. That fact could be deduced from the smacking of his lips, the sound of which reached Liza's ears. He was wearing a brown dressing-gown with black flowers on it. Massive tassels fell down to the ground. It was the first time in her life Liza had seen her husband in a dressing-gown, and such an expensive-looking one.

Mishutka was sitting on one of his knees, and hindering him from drinking his tea. The child jumped up and down and tried to clutch his papa's shining lip. After every three or four sips the father bent down to his son and kissed him on the head. A grey cat with its tail in the air was rubbing itself against one of the table legs, and with a plaintive mew proclaiming its desire for food. Liza hid behind the verandah curtain, and fastened her eyes upon the members of her former family; her face was radiant with joy.

"Misha!" she murmured, "Misha! Are you really here, Misha? The darling! And how he loves Vanya! Heavens!"

And Liza went off into a giggle when Mishutka stirred his father's tea with a spoon. "And how Vanya loves Misha! My darlings!"

Liza's heart throbbed, and her head went round with joy and happiness. She sank into an armchair and went on observing them, sitting down.

"How did they come here?" she wondered as she sent airy kisses to Mishutka. "Who gave them the idea of coming here? Heavens! Can all that wealth belong to them? Can those swan-like horses that were led in at the gate belong to Ivan Petrovitch? Ah!"

When he had finished his tea, Ivan Petrovitch went into the house. Ten minutes later, he appeared on the steps and Liza was astounded. . . He, who in his youth only seven years ago had been called Vanushka and Vanka and had been ready to punch a man in the face and turn the house upside down over twenty kopecks, was dressed devilishly well. He had on a broad-brimmed straw hat, exquisite brilliant boots, a piqué waistcoat. . . Thousands of suns, big and little, glistened on his watch-chain. With much *chic* he held in his right hand his gloves and cane.

And what swagger, what style there was in his heavy figure when, with a graceful motion of his hand, he bade the footman bring the horse round.

He got into the chaise with dignity, and told the footmen standing round the chaise to give him Mishutka and the fishing tackle they had brought. Setting Mishutka beside him, and putting his left arm round him, he held the reins and drove off.

"Ge-ee up!" shouted Mishutka.

Liza, unaware of what she was doing, waved her handkerchief after them. If she had looked in the glass she would have been surprised at her flushed, laughing, and, at the same time, tear-stained face. She was vexed that she was not beside her gleeful boy, and that she could not for some reason shower kisses on him at once.

For some reason! . . . Away with all your petty delicacies!

"Grisha! Grisha!" Liza ran into Groholsky's bedroom and set to work to wake him. "Get up, they have come! The darling!"

"Who has come?" asked Groholsky, waking up.

"Our people. . . Vanya and Misha, they have come, they are in the villa opposite. . . I looked out, and there they were drinking tea. . . And Misha too. . . What a little angel our Misha has grown! If only you had seen him! Mother of God!"

"Seen whom? Why, you are. . . Who has come? Come where?"

"Vanya and Misha. . . I have been looking at the villa opposite, while they were sitting drinking tea. Misha can drink his tea by himself now. . . Didn't you see them moving in yesterday, it was they who arrived!"

Groholsky rubbed his forehead and turned pale.

"Arrived? Your husband?" he asked.

"Why, yes."

"What for?"

"Most likely he is going to live here. They don't know we are here. If they did, they would have looked at our villa, but they drank their tea and took no notice."

"Where is he now? But for God's sake do talk sense! Oh, where is he?"

"He has gone fishing with Misha in the chaise. Did you see the horses yesterday? Those are their horses. . . Vanya's. . . Vanya drives with them. Do you know what, Grisha? We will have Misha to stay with us. . . We will, won't we? He is such a pretty boy. Such an exquisite boy!"

Groholsky pondered, while Liza went on talking and talking.

"This is an unexpected meeting," said Groholsky, after prolonged and, as usual, harrassing reflection. "Well, who could have expected that we should meet here? Well. . . There it is. . . So be it. It seems that it is fated. I can imagine the awkwardness of his position when he meets us."

"Shall we have Misha to stay with us?"

"Yes, we will. . . It will be awkward meeting him. . . Why, what can I say to him? What can I talk of? It will be awkward for him and awkward for me. . . We ought not to meet. We will carry on communications, if necessary, through the servants. . . My head does ache so, Lizotchka. My arms and legs too, I ache all over. Is my head feverish?"

Liza put her hand on his forehead and found that his head was hot.

"I had dreadful dreams all night. . . I shan't get up to-day. I shall stay in bed. . . I must take some quinine. Send me my breakfast here, little woman."

Groholsky took quinine and lay in bed the whole day. He drank warm water, moaned, had the sheets and pillowcase changed, whimpered, and induced an agonising boredom in all surrounding him.

He was insupportable when he imagined he had caught a chill. Liza had continually to interrupt her inquisitive observations and run from the verandah to his room. At dinner-time she had to put on mustard plasters. How boring all this would have been, O reader, if the villa opposite had not been at the service of my heroine! Liza watched that villa all day long and was gasping with happiness.

At ten o'clock Ivan Petrovitch and Mishutka came back from fishing and had breakfast. At two o'clock they had dinner, and at four o'clock they drove off somewhere in a carriage. The white horses bore them away with the swiftness of lightning. At seven o'clock visitors came to see them—all of them men. They were playing cards on two tables in the verandah till midnight. One of the men played superbly on the piano. The visitors played, ate, drank, and laughed. Ivan Petrovitch guffawing loudly, told them an anecdote of Armenian life at the top of his voice, so that all the villas round could hear. It was very gay and Mishutka sat up with them till midnight.

"Misha is merry, he is not crying," thought Liza, "so he does not remember his mamma. So he has forgotten me!"

And there was a horrible bitter feeling in Liza's soul. She spent the whole night crying. She was fretted by her little conscience, and by vexation and misery, and the desire to talk to Mishutka and kiss him. . . In the morning she got up with a headache and tear-stained eyes. Her tears Groholsky put down to his own account.

"Do not weep, darling," he said to her, "I am all right to-day, my chest is a little painful, but that is nothing."

While they were having tea, lunch was being served at the villa opposite. Ivan Petrovitch was looking at his plate, and seeing nothing but a morsel of goose dripping with fat.

"I am very glad," said Groholsky, looking askance at Bugrov, "very glad that his life is so tolerable! I hope that decent surroundings anyway may help to stifle his grief. Keep out of sight, Liza! They will see you. . . I am not disposed to talk to him just now. . . God be with him! Why trouble his peace?"

But the dinner did not pass off so quietly. During dinner precisely that "awkward position" which Groholsky so dreaded occurred. Just when the partridges, Groholsky's favorite dish, had been put on the table, Liza was suddenly overcome with confusion, and Groholsky began wiping his face with his dinner napkin. On the verandah of the villa opposite they saw Bugrov. He was standing with his arms leaning on the parapet, and staring straight at them, with his eyes starting out of his head.

"Go in, Liza, go in," Groholsky whispered. "I said we must have dinner indoors! What a girl you are, really. . ."

Bugrov stared and stared, and suddenly began shouting. Groholsky looked at him and saw a face full of astonishment. . .

"Is that you?" bawled Ivan Petrovitch, "you! Are you here too?"

Groholsky passed his fingers from one shoulder to another, as though to say, "My chest is weak, and so I can't shout across such a distance." Liza's heart began throbbing, and everything turned round before her eyes. Bugrov ran from his verandah, ran across the road, and a few seconds later was standing under the verandah on which Groholsky and Liza were dining. Alas for the partridges!

"How are you?" he began, flushing crimson, and stuffing his big hands in his pockets. "Are you here? Are you here too?"

"Yes, we are here too. . ."

"How did you get here?"

"Why, how did you?"

"I? It's a long story, a regular romance, my good friend! But don't put yourselves out—eat your dinner! I've been living, you know, ever since then. . . in the Oryol province. I rented an estate. A splendid estate! But do eat your dinner! I stayed there from the end of May, but now I have given it up. . . It was cold there, and—well, the doctor advised me to go to the Crimea. . ."

"Are you ill, then?" inquired Groholsky.

"Oh, well. . . There always seems, as it were. . . something gurgling here. . ."

And at the word "here" Ivan Petrovitch passed his open hand from his neck down to the middle of his stomach.

"So you are here too. . . Yes. . . that's very pleasant. Have you been here long?"

"Since July."

"Oh, and you, Liza, how are you? Quite well?"

"Quite well," answered Liza, and was embarrassed.

"You miss Mishutka, I'll be bound. Eh? Well, he's here with me. . . I'll send him over to you directly with Nikifor. This is very nice. Well, good-bye! I have to go off directly. . . I made the acquaintance of Prince Ter-Haimazov yesterday; delightful man, though he is an Armenian. So he has a croquet party to-day; we are going to play croquet. . . Good-bye! The carriage is waiting. . ."

Ivan Petrovitch whirled round, tossed his head, and, waving adieu to them, ran home.

"Unhappy man," said Groholsky, heaving a deep sigh as he watched him go off.

"In what way is he unhappy?" asked Liza.

"To see you and not have the right to call you his!"

"Fool!" Liza was so bold to think. "Idiot!"

Before evening Liza was hugging and kissing Mishutka. At first the boy howled, but when he was offered jam, he was all friendly smiles.

For three days Groholsky and Liza did not see Bugrov. He had disappeared somewhere, and was only at home at night. On the fourth day he visited them again at dinner-time. He came in, shook hands with both of them, and sat down to the table. His face was serious.

"I have come to you on business," he said. "Read this." And he handed Groholsky a letter. "Read it! Read it aloud!"

Groholsky read as follows:

My beloved and consoling, never-forgotten son Ioann! I have received the respectful and loving letter in which you invite your aged father to the mild and salubrious Crimea, to breathe the fragrant air, and behold strange lands. To that letter I reply that on taking my holiday, I will come to you, but not for long. My colleague, Father Gerasim, is a frail and delicate man, and cannot be left alone for long. I am very sensible of your not forgetting your parents, your father and your mother. . . You rejoice your father with your affection, and you remember your mother in your prayers, and so it is fitting to do. Meet me at Feodosia. What sort of town is Feodosia—what is it like? It will be very agreeable to see it. Your godmother, who took you from the font, is called

Feodosia. You write that God has been graciously pleased that you should win two hundred thousand roubles. That is gratifying to me. But I cannot approve of your having left the service while still of a grade of little importance; even a rich man ought to be in the service. I bless you always, now and hereafter. Ilya and Seryozhka Andronov send you their greetings. You might send them ten roubles each—they are badly off!

Your loving Father,
Pyotr Bugrov, *Priest*

Groholsky read this letter aloud, and he and Liza both looked inquiringly at Bugrov.

"You see what it is," Ivan Petrovitch began hesitatingly. "I should like to ask you, Liza, not to let him see you, to keep out of his sight while he is here. I have written to him that you are ill and gone to the Caucasus for a cure. If you meet him. . . You see yourself. . . It's awkward. . . H'm. . ."

"Very well," said Liza.

"We can do that," thought Groholsky, "since he makes sacrifices, why shouldn't we?"

"Please do. . . If he sees you there will be trouble. . . My father is a man of strict principles. He would curse me in seven churches. Don't go out of doors, Liza, that is all. He won't be here long. Don't be afraid."

Father Pyotr did not long keep them waiting. One fine morning Ivan Petrovitch ran in and hissed in a mysterious tone:

"He has come! He is asleep now, so please be careful."

And Liza was shut up within four walls. She did not venture to go out into the yard or on to the verandah. She could only see the sky from behind the window curtain. Unluckily for her, Ivan Petrovitch's papa spent his whole time in the open air, and even slept on the verandah. Usually Father Pyotr, a little parish priest, in a brown cassock and a top hat with a curly brim, walked slowly round the villas and gazed with curiosity at the "strange lands" through his grandfatherly spectacles. Ivan Petrovitch with the Stanislav on a little ribbon accompanied him. He did not wear a decoration as a rule, but before his own people he liked to show off. In their society he always wore the Stanislav.

Liza was bored to death. Groholsky suffered too. He had to go for his walks alone without a companion. He almost shed tears, but. . . had to submit to his fate. And to make things worse, Bugrov would run across every morning and in a hissing whisper would give some quite unnecessary bulletin concerning the health of Father Pyotr. He bored them with those bulletins.

"He slept well," he informed them. "Yesterday he was put out because I had no salted cucumbers. . . He has taken to Mishutka; he keeps patting him on the head."

At last, a fortnight later, little Father Pyotr walked for the last time round the villas and, to Groholsky's immense relief, departed. He had enjoyed himself, and went off very well satisfied. Liza and Groholsky fell back into their old manner of life. Groholsky once more blessed his fate. But his happiness did not last for long. A new trouble worse than Father Pyotr followed. Ivan Petrovitch took to coming to see them every day. Ivan Petrovitch, to be frank, though a capital fellow, was a very tedious person. He came at dinner-time, dined with them and stayed a very long time. That would not have mattered. But they had to buy vodka, which Groholsky could not endure, for his dinner. He would drink five glasses and talk the whole dinner-time. That, too, would not have mattered. . . But he would sit on till two o'clock in the morning, and not let them get to bed, and, worse still, he permitted himself to talk of things about which he should have been silent. When towards two o'clock in the morning he had drunk too much vodka and champagne, he would take Mishutka in his arms, and weeping, say to him, before Groholsky and Liza:

"Mihail, my son, what am I? I. . . am a scoundrel. I have sold your mother! Sold her for thirty pieces of silver, may the Lord punish me! Mihail Ivanitch, little sucking pig, where is your mother? Lost! Gone! Sold into slavery! Well, I am a scoundrel."

These tears and these words turned Groholsky's soul inside out. He would look timidly at Liza's pale face and wring his hands.

"Go to bed, Ivan Petrovitch," he would say timidly.

"I am going. . . Come along, Mishutka. . . The Lord be our judge! I cannot think of sleep while I know that my wife is a slave. . . But it is not Groholsky's fault. . . The goods were mine, the money his. . . Freedom for the free and Heaven for the saved."

By day Ivan Petrovitch was no less insufferable to Groholsky. To Groholsky's intense horror, he was always at Liza's side. He went fishing with her, told her stories, walked with her, and even on one occasion, taking advantage of Groholsky's having a cold, carried her off in his carriage, goodness knows where, and did not bring her back till night!

"It's outrageous, inhuman," thought Groholsky, biting his lips.

Groholsky liked to be continually kissing Liza. He could not exist without those honeyed kisses, and it was awkward to kiss her before Ivan Petrovitch. It was agony. The poor fellow felt forlorn, but fate soon had compassion on him. Ivan Petrovitch suddenly went off somewhere for a whole week. Visitors had come and carried him off with them. . . And Mishutka was taken too.

One fine morning Groholsky came home from a walk good-humoured and beaming.

"He has come," he said to Liza, rubbing his hands. "I am very glad he has come. Ha-ha-ha!"

"What are you laughing at?"

"There are women with him."

"What women?"

"I don't know. . . It's a good thing he has got women. . . A capital thing, in fact. . . He is still young and fresh. Come here! Look!"

Groholsky led Liza on to the verandah, and pointed to the villa opposite. They both held their sides, and roared with laughter. It was funny. Ivan Petrovitch was standing on the verandah of the villa opposite, smiling. Two dark-haired ladies and Mishutka were standing below, under the verandah. The ladies were laughing, and loudly talking French.

"French women," observed Groholsky. "The one nearest us isn't at all bad-looking. Lively damsels, but that's no matter. There are good women to be found even among such. . . But they really do go too far."

What was funny was that Ivan Petrovitch bent across the verandah, and stretching with his long arms, put them round the shoulders of one of the French girls, lifted her in the air, and set her giggling on the verandah. After lifting up both ladies on to the verandah, he lifted up Mishutka too. The ladies ran down and the proceedings were repeated.

"Powerful muscles, I must say," muttered Groholsky looking at this scene. The operation was repeated some six times, the ladies were so amiable as to show no embarrassment whatever when the boisterous wind disposed of their inflated skirts as it willed while they were being lifted. Groholsky dropped his eyes in a shamefaced way when the ladies flung their legs over the parapet as they reached the verandah. But Liza watched and laughed! What did she care? It was not a case of men misbehaving themselves, which would have put her, as a woman, to shame, but of ladies.

In the evening, Ivan Petrovitch flew over, and with some embarrassment announced that he was now a man with a household to look after. . .

"You mustn't imagine they are just anybody," he said. "It is true they are French. They shout at the top of their voices, and drink. . . but we all know! The French are brought up to be like that! It can't be helped. . . The prince," Ivan Petrovitch added, "let me have them almost for nothing. . . He said: 'take them, take them. . .' I must introduce you to the prince sometime. A man of culture! He's for ever writing, writing. . . And do you know what their names are? One is Fanny, the other Isabella. . . There's Europe, ha-ha-ha! . . . The west! Good-bye!"

Ivan Petrovitch left Liza and Groholsky in peace, and devoted himself to his ladies. All day long sound of talk, laughter, and the clatter of crockery came from his villa. . . The lights were not put out till far into the night. . . Groholsky was in bliss. . . At last, after a prolonged interval of agony, he felt happy and at peace again. Ivan Petrovitch with his two ladies had no such happiness as he had with one. But alas, destiny has no heart. She plays with the Groholskys, the Lizas, the Ivans, and the Mishutkas as with pawns. . . Groholsky lost his peace again. . .

One morning, about ten days afterwards, on waking up late, he went out on to the verandah and saw a spectacle which shocked him, revolted him, and moved him to intense indignation. Under the verandah of the villa opposite stood the French women, and between them Liza. She was talking and looking askance at her own villa as though to see whether that tyrant, that despot were awake (so Groholsky interpreted those looks). Ivan Petrovitch standing on the verandah with his sleeves tucked up, lifted Isabella into the air, then Fanny, and then Liza. When he was lifting Liza it seemed to Groholsky that he pressed her to himself. . . Liza too flung one leg over the parapet. . . Oh these women! All sphinxes, every one of them!

When Liza returned home from her husband's villa and went into the bedroom on tip-toe, as though nothing had happened, Groholsky, pale, with hectic flushes on his cheeks, was lying in the attitude of a man at his last gasp and moaning.

On seeing Liza, he sprang out of bed, and began pacing about the bedroom.

"So that's what you are like, is it?" he shrieked in a high tenor. "So that's it! Very much obliged to you! It's revolting, madam! Immoral, in fact! Let me tell you that!"

Liza turned pale, and of course burst into tears. When women feel that they are in the right, they scold and shed tears; when they are conscious of being in fault, they shed tears only.

"On a level with those depraved creatures! It's... it's... it's... lower than any impropriety! Why, do you know what they are? They are kept women! Cocottes! And you a respectable woman go rushing off where they are... And he... He! What does he want? What more does he want of me? I don't understand it! I have given him half of my property—I have given him more! You know it yourself! I have given him what I have not myself... I have given him almost all... And he! I've put up with your calling him Vanya, though he has no right whatever to such intimacy. I have put up with your walks, kisses after dinner... I have put up with everything, but this I will not put up with... Either he or I! Let him go away, or I go away! I'm not equal to living like this any longer, no! You can see that for yourself!... Either he or I... Enough! The cup is brimming over... I have suffered a great deal as it is... I am going to talk to him at once—this minute! What is he, after all? What has he to be proud of? No, indeed... He has no reason to think so much of himself..."

Groholsky said a great many more valiant and stinging things, but did not "go at once"; he felt timid and abashed... He went to Ivan Petrovitch three days later.

When he went into his apartment, he gaped with astonishment. He was amazed at the wealth and luxury with which Bugrov had surrounded himself. Velvet hangings, fearfully expensive chairs... One was positively ashamed to step on the carpet. Groholsky had seen many rich men in his day, but he had never seen such frenzied luxury... And the higgledy-piggledy muddle he saw when, with an inexplicable tremor, he walked into the drawing-room—plates with bits of bread on them were lying about on the grand piano, a glass was standing on a chair, under the table there was a basket with a filthy rag in it... Nut shells were strewn about in the windows. Bugrov himself was not quite in his usual trim when Groholsky walked in... With a red face and uncombed locks he was pacing about the room in deshabille, talking to himself, apparently much agitated. Mishutka was sitting on the sofa there in the drawing-room, and was making the air vibrate with a piercing scream.

"It's awful, Grigory Vassilyevitch!" Bugrov began on seeing Groholsky, "such disorder. . . such disorder. . . Please sit down. You must excuse my being in the costume of Adam and Eve. . . It's of no consequence. . . Horrible disorderliness! I don't understand how people can exist here, I don't understand it! The servants won't do what they are told, the climate is horrible, everything is expensive. . . Stop your noise," Bugrov shouted, suddenly coming to a halt before Mishutka; "stop it, I tell you! Little beast, won't you stop it?"

And Bugrov pulled Mishutka's ear.

"That's revolting, Ivan Petrovitch," said Groholsky in a tearful voice. "How can you treat a tiny child like that? You really are. . ."

"Let him stop yelling then. . . Be quiet—I'll whip you!"

"Don't cry, Misha darling. . . Papa won't touch you again. Don't beat him, Ivan Petrovitch; why, he is hardly more than a baby. . . There, there. . . Would you like a little horse? I'll send you a little horse. . . You really are hard-hearted. . ."

Groholsky paused, and then asked:

"And how are your ladies getting on, Ivan Petrovitch?"

"Not at all. I've turned them out without ceremony. I might have gone on keeping them, but it's awkward. . . The boy will grow up. . . A father's example. . . If I were alone, then it would be a different thing. . . Besides, what's the use of my keeping them? Poof. . . it's a regular farce! I talk to them in Russian, and they answer me in French. They don't understand a thing—you can't knock anything into their heads."

"I've come to you about something, Ivan Petrovitch, to talk things over. . . H'm. . . It's nothing very particular. But just. . . two or three words. . . In reality, I have a favour to ask of you."

"What's that?"

"Would you think it possible, Ivan Petrovitch, to go away? We are delighted that you are here; it's very agreeable for us, but it's inconvenient, don't you know. . . You will understand me. It's awkward in a way. . . Such indefinite relations, such continual awkwardness in regard to one another. . . We must part. . . It's essential in fact. Excuse my saying so, but. . . you must see for yourself, of course, that in such circumstances to be living side by side leads to. . . reflections. . . that is. . . not to reflections, but there is a certain awkward feeling. . ."

"Yes. . . That is so, I have thought of it myself. Very good, I will go away."

"We shall be very grateful to you. . . Believe me, Ivan Petrovitch, we shall preserve the most flattering memory of you. The sacrifice which you. . ."

"Very good. . . Only what am I to do with all this? I say, you buy this furniture of mine! What do you say? It's not expensive, eight thousand. . . ten. . . The furniture, the carriage, the grand piano. . ."

"Very good. . . I will give you ten thousand. . ."

"Well, that is capital! I will set off to-morrow. I shall go to Moscow. It's impossible to live here. Everything is so dear! Awfully dear! The money fairly flies. . . You can't take a step without spending a thousand! I can't go on like that. I have a child to bring up. . . Well, thank God that you will buy my furniture. . . That will be a little more in hand, or I should have been regularly bankrupt. . ."

Groholsky got up, took leave of Bugrov, and went home rejoicing. In the evening he sent him ten thousand roubles.

Early next morning Bugrov and Mishutka were already at Feodosia.

III

SEVERAL MONTHS HAD PASSED; SPRING had come. With spring, fine bright days had come too. Life was not so dull and hateful, and the earth was more fair to look upon. . . There was a warm breeze from the sea and the open country. . . The earth was covered with fresh grass, fresh leaves were green upon the trees. Nature had sprung into new life, and had put on new array.

It might be thought that new hopes and new desires would surge up in man when everything in nature is renewed, and young and fresh. . . but it is hard for man to renew life. . .

Groholsky was still living in the same villa. His hopes and desires, small and unexacting, were still concentrated on the same Liza, on her alone, and on nothing else! As before, he could not take his eyes off her, and gloated over the thought: how happy I am! The poor fellow really did feel awfully happy. Liza sat as before on the verandah, and unaccountably stared with bored eyes at the villa opposite and the trees near it through which there was a peep at the dark blue sea. . . As before, she spent her days for the most part in silence, often in tears and from time to time in putting mustard plasters on Groholsky. She might be congratulated on one new sensation, however. There was a worm gnawing at her vitals. . . That worm was misery. . . She was fearfully miserable, pining for her son, for her old, her cheerful manner of life.

Her life in the past had not been particularly cheerful, but still it was livelier than her present existence. When she lived with her husband she used from time to time to go to a theatre, to an entertainment, to visit acquaintances. But here with Groholsky it was all quietness and emptiness. . . Besides, here there was one man, and he with his ailments and his continual mawkish kisses, was like an old grandfather for ever shedding tears of joy.

It was boring! Here she had not Mihey Sergeyitch who used to be fond of dancing the mazurka with her. She had not Spiridon Nikolaitch, the son of the editor of the *Provincial News*. Spiridon Nikolaitch sang well and recited poetry. Here she had not a table set with lunch for visitors. She had not Gerasimovna, the old nurse who used to be continually grumbling at her for eating too much jam. . . She had no one! There was simply nothing for her but to lie down and die of depression. Groholsky rejoiced in his solitude, but. . . he was wrong to rejoice in it. All too soon he paid for his egoism. At the beginning of May when the very air seemed to be in love and faint with happiness, Groholsky lost everything; the woman he loved and. . .

That year Bugrov, too, visited the Crimea. He did not take the villa opposite, but pottered about, going from one town to another with Mishutka. He spent his time eating, drinking, sleeping, and playing cards. He had lost all relish for fishing, shooting and the French women, who, between ourselves, had robbed him a bit. He had grown thin, lost his broad and beaming smiles, and had taken to dressing in canvas. Ivan Petrovitch from time to time visited Groholsky's villa. He brought Liza jam, sweets, and fruit, and seemed trying to dispel her ennui. Groholsky was not troubled by these visits, especially as they were brief and infrequent, and were apparently paid on account of Mishutka, who could not under any circumstances have been altogether deprived of the privilege of seeing his mother. Bugrov came, unpacked his presents, and after saying a few words, departed. And those few words he said not to Liza but to Groholsky. . . With Liza he was silent and Groholsky's mind was at rest; but there is a Russian proverb which he would have done well to remember: "Don't fear the dog that barks, but fear the dog that's quiet. . ." A fiendish proverb, but in practical life sometimes indispensable.

As he was walking in the garden one day, Groholsky heard two voices in conversation. One voice was a man's, the other was a woman's. One belonged to Bugrov, the other to Liza. Groholsky listened, and turning white as death, turned softly towards the speakers. He halted behind a lilac bush, and proceeded to watch and listen. His arms and legs turned cold. A cold sweat came out upon his brow. He clutched several branches of the lilac that he might not stagger and fall down. All was over!

Bugrov had his arm round Liza's waist, and was saying to her:

"My darling! what are we to do? It seems it was God's will. . . I am a scoundrel. . . I sold you. I was seduced by that Herod's money, plague take him, and what good have I had from the money? Nothing but anxiety and display! No peace, no happiness, no position. . . One sits like a fat invalid at the same spot, and never a step forwarder. . . Have you heard that Andrushka Markuzin has been made a head clerk? Andrushka, that fool! While I stagnate. . . Good heavens! I have lost you, I have lost my happiness. I am a scoundrel, a blackguard, how do you think I shall feel at the dread day of judgment?"

"Let us go away, Vanya," wailed Liza. "I am dull. . . I am dying of depression."

"We cannot, the money has been taken. . ."

"Well, give it back again."

"I should be glad to, but. . . wait a minute. I have spent it all. We must submit, my girl. God is chastising us. Me for my covetousness and you for your frivolity. Well, let us be tortured. . . It will be the better for us in the next world."

And in an access of religious feeling, Bugrov turned up his eyes to heaven.

"But I cannot go on living here; I am miserable."

"Well, there is no help for it. I'm miserable too. Do you suppose I am happy without you? I am pining and wasting away! And my chest has begun to be bad! . . . You are my lawful wife, flesh of my flesh. . . one flesh. . . You must live and bear it! While I. . . will drive over. . . visit you."

And bending down to Liza, Bugrov whispered, loudly enough, however, to be heard several yards away:

"I will come to you at night, Lizanka. . . Don't worry. . . I am staying at Feodosia close by. . . I will live here near you till I have run through everything. . . and I soon shall be at my last farthing! A-a-ah, what a life it is! Dreariness, ill. . . my chest is bad, and my stomach is bad."

Bugrov ceased speaking, and then it was Liza's turn. . . My God, the cruelty of that woman! She began weeping, complaining, enumerating all the defects of her lover and her own sufferings. Groholsky as he listened to her, felt that he was a villain, a miscreant, a murderer.

"He makes me miserable. . ." Liza said in conclusion.

After kissing Liza at parting, and going out at the garden gate, Bugrov came upon Groholsky, who was standing at the gate waiting for him.

"Ivan Petrovitch," said Groholsky in the tone of a dying man, "I have seen and heard it all. . . It's not honourable on your part, but I do not blame you. . . You love her too, but you must understand that she is mine. Mine! I cannot live without her! How is it you don't understand that? Granted that you love her, that you are miserable. . . Have I not paid you, in part at least, for your sufferings? For God's sake, go away! For God's sake, go away! Go away from here for ever, I implore you, or you will kill me. . ."

"I have nowhere to go," Bugrov said thickly.

"H'm, you have squandered everything. . . You are an impulsive man. Very well. . . Go to my estate in the province of Tchernigov. If you like I will make you a present of the property. It's a small estate, but a good one. . . On my honour, it's a good one!"

Bugrov gave a broad grin. He suddenly felt himself in the seventh heaven.

"I will give it you. . . This very day I will write to my steward and send him an authorisation for completing the purchase. You must tell everyone you have bought it. . . Go away, I entreat you."

"Very good, I will go. I understand."

"Let us go to a notary. . . at once," said Groholsky, greatly cheered, and he went to order the carriage.

On the following evening, when Liza was sitting on the garden seat where her rendezvous with Ivan Petrovitch usually took place, Groholsky went quietly to her. He sat down beside her, and took her hand.

"Are you dull, Lizotchka?" he said, after a brief silence. "Are you depressed? Why shouldn't we go away somewhere? Why is it we always stay at home? We want to go about, to enjoy ourselves, to make acquaintances. . . Don't we?"

"I want nothing," said Liza, and turned her pale, thin face towards the path by which Bugrov used to come to her.

Groholsky pondered. He knew who it was she expected, who it was she wanted.

"Let us go home, Liza," he said, "it is damp here. . ."

"You go; I'll come directly."

Groholsky pondered again.

"You are expecting him?" he asked, and made a wry face as though his heart had been gripped with red-hot pincers.

"Yes. . . I want to give him the socks for Misha. . ."

"He will not come."

"How do you know?"

"He has gone away. . ."

Liza opened her eyes wide. . .

"He has gone away, gone to the Tchernigov province. I have given him my estate. . ."

Liza turned fearfully pale, and caught at Groholsky's shoulder to save herself from falling.

"I saw him off at the steamer at three o'clock."

Liza suddenly clutched at her head, made a movement, and falling on the seat, began shaking all over.

"Vanya," she wailed, "Vanya! I will go to Vanya. . . Darling!"

She had a fit of hysterics. . .

And from that evening, right up to July, two shadows could be seen in the park in which the summer visitors took their walks. The shadows wandered about from morning till evening, and made the summer visitors feel dismal. . . After Liza's shadow invariably walked the shadow of Groholsky. . . I call them shadows because they had both lost their natural appearance. They had grown thin and pale and shrunken, and looked more like shadows than living people. . . Both were pining away like fleas in the classic anecdote of the Jew who sold insect powder.

At the beginning of July, Liza ran away from Groholsky, leaving a note in which she wrote that she was going for a time to "her son" . . . For a time! She ran away by night when Groholsky was asleep. . . After reading her letter Groholsky spent a whole week wandering round about the villa as though he were mad, and neither ate nor slept. In August, he had an attack of recurrent fever, and in September he went abroad. There he took to drink. . . He hoped in drink and dissipation to find comfort. . . He squandered all his fortune, but did not succeed, poor fellow, in driving out of his brain the image of the beloved woman with the kittenish face. . . Men do not die of happiness, nor do they die of misery. Groholsky's hair went grey, but he did not die: he is alive to this day. . . He came back from abroad to have "just a peep" at Liza. . .

Bugrov met him with open arms, and made him stay for an indefinite period. He is staying with Bugrov to this day.

This year I happened to be passing through Groholyovka, Bugrov's estate. I found the master and the mistress of the house having supper. . . Ivan Petrovitch was highly delighted to see me, and fell to pressing good things upon me. . . He had grown rather stout, and his face was a trifle puffy, though it was still rosy and looked sleek and well-nourished. . . He was not bald. Liza, too, had grown fatter. Plumpness did not suit her. Her face was beginning to lose the kittenish look, and was, alas! more suggestive of the seal. Her cheeks were spreading upwards, outwards, and to both sides. The Bugrovs were living in first-rate style. They had plenty of everything. The house was overflowing with servants and edibles. . .

When we had finished supper we got into conversation. Forgetting that Liza did not play, I asked her to play us something on the piano.

"She does not play," said Bugrov; "she is no musician. . . Hey, you there! Ivan! call Grigory Vassilyevitch here! What's he doing there?" And turning to me, Bugrov added, "Our musician will come directly; he plays the guitar. We keep the piano for Mishutka—we are having him taught. . ."

Five minutes later, Groholsky walked into the room—sleepy, unkempt, and unshaven. . . He walked in, bowed to me, and sat down on one side.

"Why, whoever goes to bed so early?" said Bugrov, addressing him. "What a fellow you are really! He's always asleep, always asleep. . . The sleepy head! Come, play us something lively. . ."

Groholsky turned the guitar, touched the strings, and began singing:

"Yesterday I waited for my dear one. . ."

I listened to the singing, looked at Bugrov's well-fed countenance, and thought: "Nasty brute!" I felt like crying. . . When he had finished singing, Groholsky bowed to us, and went out.

"And what am I to do with him?" Bugrov said when he had gone away. "I do have trouble with him! In the day he is always brooding and brooding. . . And at night he moans. . . He sleeps, but he sighs and moans in his sleep. . . It is a sort of illness. . . What am I to do with him, I can't think! He won't let us sleep. . . I am afraid that he will go out of his mind. People think he is badly treated here. . . In what way is he badly treated? He eats with us, and he drinks with us. . . Only we won't give him money. If we were to give him any he would spend it on drink or waste it. . . That's another trouble for me! Lord forgive me, a sinner!"

They made me stay the night. When I woke next morning, Bugrov was giving some one a lecture in the adjoining room. . .

"Set a fool to say his prayers, and he will crack his skull on the floor! Why, who paints oars green! Do think, blockhead! Use your sense! Why don't you speak?"

"I. . . I. . . made a mistake," said a husky tenor apologetically.

The tenor belonged to Groholsky.

Groholsky saw me to the station.

"He is a despot, a tyrant," he kept whispering to me all the way. "He is a generous man, but a tyrant! Neither heart nor brain are developed in him. . . He tortures me! If it were not for that noble woman, I should have gone away long ago. I am sorry to leave her. It's somehow easier to endure together."

Groholsky heaved a sigh, and went on:

"She is with child. . . You notice it? It is really my child. . . Mine. . . She soon saw her mistake, and gave herself to me again. She cannot endure him. . ."

"You are a rag," I could not refrain from saying to Groholsky.

"Yes, I am a man of weak character. . . That is quite true. I was born so. Do you know how I came into the world? My late papa cruelly oppressed a certain little clerk—it was awful how he treated him! He poisoned his life. Well. . . and my late mama was tender-hearted. She came from the people, she was of the working class. . . She took that little clerk to her heart from pity. . . Well. . . and so I came into the world. . . The son of the ill-treated clerk. How could I have a strong will? Where was I to get it from? But that's the second bell. . . Goodbye. Come and see us again, but don't tell Ivan Petrovitch what I have said about him."

I pressed Groholsky's hand, and got into the train. He bowed towards the carriage, and went to the water-barrel—I suppose he was thirsty!

The Doctor

It was still in the drawing-room, so still that a house-fly that had flown in from outside could be distinctly heard brushing against the ceiling. Olga Ivanovna, the lady of the villa, was standing by the window, looking out at the flower-beds and thinking. Dr. Tsvyetkov, who was her doctor as well as an old friend, and had been sent for to treat her son Misha, was sitting in an easy chair and swinging his hat, which he held in both hands, and he too was thinking. Except them, there was not a soul in the drawing-room or in the adjoining rooms. The sun had set, and the shades of evening began settling in the corners under the furniture and on the cornices.

The silence was broken by Olga Ivanovna.

"No misfortune more terrible can be imagined," she said, without turning from the window. "You know that life has no value for me whatever apart from the boy."

"Yes, I know that," said the doctor.

"No value whatever," said Olga Ivanovna, and her voice quivered. "He is everything to me. He is my joy, my happiness, my wealth. And if, as you say, I cease to be a mother, if he. . . dies, there will be nothing left of me but a shadow. I cannot survive it."

Wringing her hands, Olga Ivanovna walked from one window to the other and went on:

"When he was born, I wanted to send him away to the Foundling Hospital, you remember that, but, my God, how can that time be compared with now? Then I was vulgar, stupid, feather-headed, but now I am a mother, do you understand? I am a mother, and that's all I care to know. Between the present and the past there is an impassable gulf."

Silence followed again. The doctor shifted his seat from the chair to the sofa and impatiently playing with his hat, kept his eyes fixed upon Olga Ivanovna. From his face it could be seen that he wanted to speak, and was waiting for a fitting moment.

"You are silent, but still I do not give up hope," said the lady, turning round. "Why are you silent?"

"I should be as glad of any hope as you, Olga, but there is none," Tsvyetkov answered, "we must look the hideous truth in the face. The boy has a tumour on the brain, and we must try to prepare ourselves for his death, for such cases never recover."

ANTON CHEKHOV

"Nikolay, are you certain you are not mistaken?"

"Such questions lead to nothing. I am ready to answer as many as you like, but it will make it no better for us."

Olga Ivanovna pressed her face into the window curtains, and began weeping bitterly. The doctor got up and walked several times up and down the drawing-room, then went to the weeping woman, and lightly touched her arm. Judging from his uncertain movements, from the expression of his gloomy face, which looked dark in the dusk of the evening, he wanted to say something.

"Listen, Olga," he began. "Spare me a minute's attention; there is something I must ask you. You can't attend to me now, though. I'll come later, afterwards. . ." He sat down again, and sank into thought. The bitter, imploring weeping, like the weeping of a little girl, continued. Without waiting for it to end, Tsvyetkov heaved a sigh and walked out of the drawing-room. He went into the nursery to Misha. The boy was lying on his back as before, staring at one point as though he were listening. The doctor sat down on his bed and felt his pulse.

"Misha, does your head ache?" he asked.

Misha answered, not at once: "Yes. I keep dreaming."

"What do you dream?"

"All sorts of things. . ."

The doctor, who did not know how to talk with weeping women or with children, stroked his burning head, and muttered:

"Never mind, poor boy, never mind. . . One can't go through life without illness. . . Misha, who am I—do you know me?"

Misha did not answer.

"Does your head ache very badly?"

"Ve-ery. I keep dreaming."

After examining him and putting a few questions to the maid who was looking after the sick child, the doctor went slowly back to the drawing-room. There it was by now dark, and Olga Ivanovna, standing by the window, looked like a silhouette.

"Shall I light up?" asked Tsvyetkov.

No answer followed. The house-fly was still brushing against the ceiling. Not a sound floated in from outside as though the whole world, like the doctor, were thinking, and could not bring itself to speak. Olga Ivanovna was not weeping now, but as before, staring at the flower-bed in profound silence. When Tsvyetkov went up to her, and through the twilight glanced at her pale face, exhausted with grief, her expression was such as he had seen before during her attacks of acute, stupefying, sick headache.

"Nikolay Trofimitch!" she addressed him, "and what do you think about a consultation?"

"Very good; I'll arrange it to-morrow."

From the doctor's tone it could be easily seen that he put little faith in the benefit of a consultation. Olga Ivanovna would have asked him something else, but her sobs prevented her. Again she pressed her face into the window curtain. At that moment, the strains of a band playing at the club floated in distinctly. They could hear not only the wind instruments, but even the violins and the flutes.

"If he is in pain, why is he silent?" asked Olga Ivanovna. "All day long, not a sound, he never complains, and never cries. I know God will take the poor boy from us because we have not known how to prize him. Such a treasure!"

The band finished the march, and a minute later began playing a lively waltz for the opening of the ball.

"Good God, can nothing really be done?" moaned Olga Ivanovna. "Nikolay, you are a doctor and ought to know what to do! You must understand that I can't bear the loss of him! I can't survive it."

The doctor, who did not know how to talk to weeping women, heaved a sigh, and paced slowly about the drawing-room. There followed a succession of oppressive pauses interspersed with weeping and the questions which lead to nothing. The band had already played a quadrille, a polka, and another quadrille. It got quite dark. In the adjoining room, the maid lighted the lamp; and all the while the doctor kept his hat in his hands, and seemed trying to say something. Several times Olga Ivanovna went off to her son, sat by him for half an hour, and came back again into the drawing-room; she was continually breaking into tears and lamentations. The time dragged agonisingly, and it seemed as though the evening had no end.

At midnight, when the band had played the cotillion and ceased altogether, the doctor got ready to go.

"I will come again to-morrow," he said, pressing the mother's cold hand. "You go to bed."

After putting on his greatcoat in the passage and picking up his walking-stick, he stopped, thought a minute, and went back into the drawing-room.

"I'll come to-morrow, Olga," he repeated in a quivering voice. "Do you hear?"

She did not answer, and it seemed as though grief had robbed her of all power of speech. In his greatcoat and with his stick still in his hand, the doctor sat down beside her, and began in a soft, tender half-whisper, which was utterly out of keeping with his heavy, dignified figure:

"Olga! For the sake of your sorrow which I share. . . Now, when falsehood is criminal, I beseech you to tell me the truth. You have always declared that the boy is my son. Is that the truth?"

Olga Ivanovna was silent.

"You have been the one attachment in my life," the doctor went on, "and you cannot imagine how deeply my feeling is wounded by falsehood. . . Come, I entreat you, Olga, for once in your life, tell me the truth. . . At these moments one cannot lie. Tell me that Misha is not my son. I am waiting."

"He is."

Olga Ivanovna's face could not be seen, but in her voice the doctor could hear hesitation. He sighed.

"Even at such moments you can bring yourself to tell a lie," he said in his ordinary voice. "There is nothing sacred to you! Do listen, do understand me. . . You have been the one only attachment in my life. Yes, you were depraved, vulgar, but I have loved no one else but you in my life. That trivial love, now that I am growing old, is the one solitary bright spot in my memories. Why do you darken it with deception? What is it for?"

"I don't understand you."

"Oh my God!" cried Tsvyetkov. "You are lying, you understand very well!" he cried more loudly, and he began pacing about the drawing-room, angrily waving his stick. "Or have you forgotten? Then I will remind you! A father's rights to the boy are equally shared with me by Petrov and Kurovsky the lawyer, who still make you an allowance for their son's education, just as I do! Yes, indeed! I know all that quite well! I forgive your lying in the past, what does it matter? But now when you have grown older, at this moment when the boy is dying, your lying stifles me! How sorry I am that I cannot speak, how sorry I am!"

The doctor unbuttoned his overcoat, and still pacing about, said:

"Wretched woman! Even such moments have no effect on her! Even now she lies as freely as nine years ago in the Hermitage Restaurant! She is afraid if she tells me the truth I shall leave off giving her money, she thinks that if she did not lie I should not love the boy! You are lying! It's contemptible!"

The doctor rapped the floor with his stick, and cried:

"It's loathsome. Warped, corrupted creature! I must despise you, and I ought to be ashamed of my feeling. Yes! Your lying has stuck in my throat these nine years, I have endured it, but now it's too much—too much."

From the dark corner where Olga Ivanovna was sitting there came the sound of weeping. The doctor ceased speaking and cleared his throat. A silence followed. The doctor slowly buttoned up his over-coat, and began looking for his hat which he had dropped as he walked about.

"I lost my temper," he muttered, bending down to the floor. "I quite lost sight of the fact that you cannot attend to me now. . . God knows what I have said. . . Don't take any notice of it, Olga."

He found his hat and went towards the dark corner.

"I have wounded you," he said in a soft, tender half-whisper, "but once more I entreat you, tell me the truth; there should not be lying between us. . . I blurted it out, and now you know that Petrov and Kurovsky are no secret to me. So now it is easy for you to tell me the truth."

Olga Ivanovna thought a moment, and with perceptible hesitation, said:

"Nikolay, I am not lying—Misha is your child."

"My God," moaned the doctor, "then I will tell you something more: I have kept your letter to Petrov in which you call him Misha's father! Olga, I know the truth, but I want to hear it from you! Do you hear?"

Olga Ivanovna made no reply, but went on weeping. After waiting for an answer the doctor shrugged his shoulders and went out.

"I will come to-morrow," he called from the passage.

All the way home, as he sat in his carriage, he was shrugging his shoulders and muttering:

"What a pity that I don't know how to speak! I haven't the gift of persuading and convincing. It's evident she does not understand me since she lies! It's evident! How can I make her see? How?"

Too Early!

The bells are ringing for service in the village of Shalmovo. The sun is already kissing the earth on the horizon; it has turned crimson and will soon disappear. In Semyon's pothouse, which has lately changed its name and become a restaurant—a title quite out of keeping with the wretched little hut with its thatch torn off its roof, and its couple of dingy windows—two peasant sportsmen are sitting. One of them is called Filimon Slyunka; he is an old man of sixty, formerly a house-serf, belonging to the Counts Zavalin, by trade a carpenter. He has at one time been employed in a nail factory, has been turned off for drunkenness and idleness, and now lives upon his old wife, who begs for alms. He is thin and weak, with a mangy-looking little beard, speaks with a hissing sound, and after every word twitches the right side of his face and jerkily shrugs his right shoulder. The other, Ignat Ryabov, a sturdy, broad-shouldered peasant who never does anything and is everlastingly silent, is sitting in the corner under a big string of bread rings. The door, opening inwards, throws a thick shadow upon him, so that Slyunka and Semyon the publican can see nothing but his patched knees, his long fleshy nose, and a big tuft of hair which has escaped from the thick uncombed tangle covering his head. Semyon, a sickly little man, with a pale face and a long sinewy neck, stands behind his counter, looks mournfully at the string of bread rings, and coughs meekly.

"You think it over now, if you have any sense," Slyunka says to him, twitching his cheek. "You have the thing lying by unused and get no sort of benefit from it. While we need it. A sportsman without a gun is like a sacristan without a voice. You ought to understand that, but I see you don't understand it, so you can have no real sense. . . Hand it over!"

"You left the gun in pledge, you know!" says Semyon in a thin womanish little voice, sighing deeply, and not taking his eyes off the string of bread rings. "Hand over the rouble you borrowed, and then take your gun."

"I haven't got a rouble. I swear to you, Semyon Mitritch, as God sees me: you give me the gun and I will go to-day with Ignashka and bring it you back again. I'll bring it back, strike me dead. May I have happiness neither in this world nor the next, if I don't."

"Semyon Mitritch, do give it," Ignat Ryabov says in his bass, and his voice betrays a passionate desire to get what he asks for.

"But what do you want the gun for?" sighs Semyon, sadly shaking his head. "What sort of shooting is there now? It's still winter outside, and no game at all but crows and jackdaws."

"Winter, indeed," says Slyunka, hooing the ash out of his pipe with his finger, "it is early yet of course, but you never can tell with the snipe. The snipe's a bird that wants watching. If you are unlucky, you may sit waiting at home, and miss his flying over, and then you must wait till autumn. . . It is a business! The snipe is not a rook. . . Last year he was flying the week before Easter, while the year before we had to wait till the week after Easter! Come, do us a favour, Semyon Mitritch, give us the gun. Make us pray for you for ever. As ill-luck would have it, Ignashka has pledged his gun for drink too. Ah, when you drink you feel nothing, but now. . . ah, I wish I had never looked at it, the cursed vodka! Truly it is the blood of Satan! Give it us, Semyon Mitritch!"

"I won't give it you," says Semyon, clasping his yellow hands on his breast as though he were going to pray. "You must act fairly, Filimonushka. . . A thing is not taken out of pawn just anyhow; you must pay the money. . . Besides, what do you want to kill birds for? What's the use? It's Lent now—you are not going to eat them."

Slyunka exchanges glances with Ryabov in embarrassment, sighs, and says: "We would only go stand-shooting."

"And what for? It's all foolishness. You are not the sort of man to spend your time in foolishness. . . Ignashka, to be sure, is a man of no understanding, God has afflicted him, but you, thank the Lord, are an old man. It's time to prepare for your end. Here, you ought to go to the midnight service."

The allusion to his age visibly stings Slyunka. He clears his throat, wrinkles up his forehead, and remains silent for a full minute.

"I say, Semyon Mitritch," he says hotly, getting up and twitching not only in his right cheek but all over his face. "It's God's truth. . . May the Almighty strike me dead, after Easter I shall get something from Stepan Kuzmitch for an axle, and I will pay you not one rouble but two! May the Lord chastise me! Before the holy image, I tell you, only give me the gun!"

"Gi-ive it," Ryabov says in his growling bass; they can hear him breathing hard, and it seems that he would like to say a great deal, but cannot find the words. "Gi-ive it."

"No, brothers, and don't ask," sighs Semyon, shaking his head mournfully. "Don't lead me into sin. I won't give you the gun. It's not the fashion for a thing to be taken out of pawn and no money paid. Besides—why this indulgence? Go your way and God bless you!"

Slyunka rubs his perspiring face with his sleeve and begins hotly swearing and entreating. He crosses himself, holds out his hands to the ikon, calls his deceased father and mother to bear witness, but Semyon sighs and meekly looks as before at the string of bread rings. In the end Ignashka Ryabov, hitherto motionless, gets up impulsively and bows down to the ground before the innkeeper, but even that has no effect on him.

"May you choke with my gun, you devil," says Slyunka, with his face twitching, and his shoulders, shrugging. "May you choke, you plague, you scoundrelly soul."

Swearing and shaking his fists, he goes out of the tavern with Ryabov and stands still in the middle of the road.

"He won't give it, the damned brute," he says, in a weeping voice, looking into Ryabov's face with an injured air.

"He won't give it," booms Ryabov.

The windows of the furthest huts, the starling cote on the tavern, the tops of the poplars, and the cross on the church are all gleaming with a bright golden flame. Now they can see only half of the sun, which, as it goes to its night's rest, is winking, shedding a crimson light, and seems laughing gleefully. Slyunka and Ryabov can see the forest lying, a dark blur, to the right of the sun, a mile and a half from the village, and tiny clouds flitting over the clear sky, and they feel that the evening will be fine and still.

"Now is just the time," says Slyunka, with his face twitching. "It would be nice to stand for an hour or two. He won't give it us, the damned brute. May he. . ."

"For stand-shooting, now is the very time. . ." Ryabov articulated, as though with an effort, stammering.

After standing still for a little they walk out of the village, without saying a word to each other, and look towards the dark streak of the forest. The whole sky above the forest is studded with moving black spots, the rooks flying home to roost. The snow, lying white here and there on the dark brown plough-land, is lightly flecked with gold by the sun.

"This time last year I went stand-shooting in Zhivki," says Slyunka, after a long silence. "I brought back three snipe."

Again there follows a silence. Both stand a long time and look towards the forest, and then lazily move and walk along the muddy road from the village.

"It's most likely the snipe haven't come yet," says Slyunka, "but may be they are here."

"Kostka says they are not here yet."

"Maybe they are not, who can tell; one year is not like another. But what mud!"

"But we ought to stand."

"To be sure we ought—why not?"

"We can stand and watch; it wouldn't be amiss to go to the forest and have a look. If they are there we will tell Kostka, or maybe get a gun ourselves and come to-morrow. What a misfortune, God forgive me. It was the devil put it in my mind to take my gun to the pothouse! I am more sorry than I can tell you, Ignashka."

Conversing thus, the sportsmen approach the forest. The sun has set and left behind it a red streak like the glow of a fire, scattered here and there with clouds; there is no catching the colours of those clouds: their edges are red, but they themselves are one minute grey, at the next lilac, at the next ashen.

In the forest, among the thick branches of fir-trees and under the birch bushes, it is dark, and only the outermost twigs on the side of the sun, with their fat buds and shining bark, stand out clearly in the air. There is a smell of thawing snow and rotting leaves. It is still; nothing stirs. From the distance comes the subsiding caw of the rooks.

"We ought to be standing in Zhivki now," whispers Slyunka, looking with awe at Ryabov; "there's good stand-shooting there."

Ryabov too looks with awe at Slyunka, with unblinking eyes and open mouth.

"A lovely time," Slyunka says in a trembling whisper. "The Lord is sending a fine spring. . . and I should think the snipe are here by now. . . Why not? The days are warm now. . . The cranes were flying in the morning, lots and lots of them."

Slyunka and Ryabov, splashing cautiously through the melting snow and sticking in the mud, walk two hundred paces along the edge of the forest and there halt. Their faces wear a look of alarm and expectation of something terrible and extraordinary. They stand like posts, do not speak nor stir, and their hands gradually fall into an attitude as though they were holding a gun at the cock. . .

ANTON CHEKHOV

A big shadow creeps from the left and envelops the earth. The dusk of evening comes on. If one looks to the right, through the bushes and tree trunks, there can be seen crimson patches of the after-glow. It is still and damp. . .

"There's no sound of them," whispers Slyunka, shrugging with the cold and sniffing with his chilly nose.

But frightened by his own whisper, he holds his finger up at some one, opens his eyes wide, and purses up his lips. There is a sound of a light snapping. The sportsmen look at each other significantly, and tell each other with their eyes that it is nothing. It is the snapping of a dry twig or a bit of bark. The shadows of evening keep growing and growing, the patches of crimson gradually grow dim, and the dampness becomes unpleasant.

The sportsmen remain standing a long time, but they see and hear nothing. Every instant they expect to see a delicate leaf float through the air, to hear a hurried call like the husky cough of a child, and the flutter of wings.

"No, not a sound," Slyunka says aloud, dropping his hands and beginning to blink. "So they have not come yet."

"It's early!"

"You are right there."

The sportsmen cannot see each other's faces, it is getting rapidly dark.

"We must wait another five days," says Slyunka, as he comes out from behind a bush with Ryabov. "It's too early!"

They go homewards, and are silent all the way.

The Cossack

Maxim Tortchakov, a farmer in southern Russia, was driving home from church with his young wife and bringing back an Easter cake which had just been blessed. The sun had not yet risen, but the east was all tinged with red and gold and had dissipated the haze which usually, in the early morning, screens the blue of the sky from the eyes. It was quiet. . . The birds were hardly yet awake. . . The corncrake uttered its clear note, and far away above a little tumulus, a sleepy kite floated, heavily flapping its wings, and no other living creature could be seen all over the steppe.

Tortchakov drove on and thought that there was no better nor happier holiday than the Feast of Christ's Resurrection. He had only lately been married, and was now keeping his first Easter with his wife. Whatever he looked at, whatever he thought about, it all seemed to him bright, joyous, and happy. He thought about his farming, and thought that it was all going well, that the furnishing of his house was all the heart could desire—there was enough of everything and all of it good; he looked at his wife, and she seemed to him lovely, kind, and gentle. He was delighted by the glow in the east, and the young grass, and his squeaking chaise, and the kite. . . And when on the way, he ran into a tavern to light his cigarette and drank a glass, he felt happier still.

"It is said, 'Great is the day,'" he chattered. "Yes, it is great! Wait a bit, Lizaveta, the sun will begin to dance. It dances every Easter. So it rejoices too!"

"It is not alive," said his wife.

"But there are people on it!" exclaimed Tortchakov, "there are really! Ivan Stepanitch told me that there are people on all the planets—on the sun, and on the moon! Truly. . . but maybe the learned men tell lies— the devil only knows! Stay, surely that's not a horse? Yes, it is!"

At the Crooked Ravine, which was just half-way on the journey home, Tortchakov and his wife saw a saddled horse standing motionless, and sniffing last year's dry grass. On a hillock beside the roadside a red-haired Cossack was sitting doubled up, looking at his feet.

"Christ is risen!" Maxim shouted to him. "Wo-o-o!"

"Truly He is risen," answered the Cossack, without raising his head.

"Where are you going?"

"Home on leave."

"Why are you sitting here, then?"

"Why. . . I have fallen ill. . . I haven't the strength to go on."

"What is wrong?"

"I ache all over."

"H'm. What a misfortune! People are keeping holiday, and you fall sick! But you should ride on to a village or an inn, what's the use of sitting here!"

The Cossack raised his head, and with big, exhausted eyes, scanned Maxim, his wife, and the horse.

"Have you come from church?" he asked.

"Yes."

"The holiday found me on the high road. It was not God's will for me to reach home. I'd get on my horse at once and ride off, but I haven't the strength. . . You might, good Christians, give a wayfarer some Easter cake to break his fast!"

"Easter cake?" Tortchakov repeated, "That we can, to be sure. . . Stay, I'll. . ."

Maxim fumbled quickly in his pockets, glanced at his wife, and said:

"I haven't a knife, nothing to cut it with. And I don't like to break it, it would spoil the whole cake. There's a problem! You look and see if you haven't a knife?"

The Cossack got up groaning, and went to his saddle to get a knife.

"What an idea," said Tortchakov's wife angrily. "I won't let you slice up the Easter cake! What should I look like, taking it home already cut! Ride on to the peasants in the village, and break your fast there!"

The wife took the napkin with the Easter cake in it out of her husband's hands and said:

"I won't allow it! One must do things properly; it's not a loaf, but a holy Easter cake. And it's a sin to cut it just anyhow."

"Well, Cossack, don't be angry," laughed Tortchakov. "The wife forbids it! Good-bye. Good luck on your journey!"

Maxim shook the reins, clicked to his horse, and the chaise rolled on squeaking. For some time his wife went on grumbling, and declaring that to cut the Easter cake before reaching home was a sin and not the proper thing. In the east the first rays of the rising sun shone out, cutting their way through the feathery clouds, and the song of the lark was heard in the sky. Now not one but three kites were hovering over the steppe at a respectful distance from one another. Grasshoppers began churring in the young grass.

When they had driven three-quarters of a mile from the Crooked Ravine, Tortchakov looked round and stared intently into the distance.

"I can't see the Cossack," he said. "Poor, dear fellow, to take it into his head to fall ill on the road. There couldn't be a worse misfortune, to have to travel and not have the strength. . . I shouldn't wonder if he dies by the roadside. We didn't give him any Easter cake, Lizaveta, and we ought to have given it. I'll be bound he wants to break his fast too."

The sun had risen, but whether it was dancing or not Tortchakov did not see. He remained silent all the way home, thinking and keeping his eyes fixed on the horse's black tail. For some unknown reason he felt overcome by depression, and not a trace of the holiday gladness was left in his heart. When he had arrived home and said, "Christ is risen" to his workmen, he grew cheerful again and began talking, but when he had sat down to break the fast and had taken a bite from his piece of Easter cake, he looked regretfully at his wife, and said:

"It wasn't right of us, Lizaveta, not to give that Cossack something to eat."

"You are a queer one, upon my word," said Lizaveta, shrugging her shoulders in surprise. "Where did you pick up such a fashion as giving away the holy Easter cake on the high road? Is it an ordinary loaf? Now that it is cut and lying on the table, let anyone eat it that likes—your Cossack too! Do you suppose I grudge it?"

"That's all right, but we ought to have given the Cossack some. . . Why, he was worse off than a beggar or an orphan. On the road, and far from home, and sick too."

Tortchakov drank half a glass of tea, and neither ate nor drank anything more. He had no appetite, the tea seemed to choke him, and he felt depressed again. After breaking their fast, his wife and he lay down to sleep. When Lizaveta woke two hours later, he was standing by the window, looking into the yard.

"Are you up already?" asked his wife.

"I somehow can't sleep. . . Ah, Lizaveta," he sighed. "We were unkind, you and I, to that Cossack!"

"Talking about that Cossack again!" yawned his wife. "You have got him on the brain."

"He has served his Tsar, shed his blood maybe, and we treated him as though he were a pig. We ought to have brought the sick man home and fed him, and we did not even give him a morsel of bread."

"Catch me letting you spoil the Easter cake for nothing! And one that has been blessed too! You would have cut it on the road, and shouldn't I have looked a fool when I got home?"

Without saying anything to his wife, Maxim went into the kitchen, wrapped a piece of cake up in a napkin, together with half a dozen eggs, and went to the labourers in the barn.

"Kuzma, put down your concertina," he said to one of them. "Saddle the bay, or Ivantchik, and ride briskly to the Crooked Ravine. There you will see a sick Cossack with a horse, so give him this. Maybe he hasn't ridden away yet."

Maxim felt cheerful again, but after waiting for Kuzma for some hours, he could bear it no longer, so he saddled a horse and went off to meet him. He met him just at the Ravine.

"Well, have you seen the Cossack?"

"I can't find him anywhere, he must have ridden on."

"H'm. . . a queer business."

Tortchakov took the bundle from Kuzma, and galloped on farther. When he reached Shustrovo he asked the peasants:

"Friends, have you seen a sick Cossack with a horse? Didn't he ride by here? A red-headed fellow on a bay horse."

The peasants looked at one another, and said they had not seen the Cossack.

"The returning postman drove by, it's true, but as for a Cossack or anyone else, there has been no such."

Maxim got home at dinner time.

"I can't get that Cossack out of my head, do what you will!" he said to his wife. "He gives me no peace. I keep thinking: what if God meant to try us, and sent some saint or angel in the form of a Cossack? It does happen, you know. It's bad, Lizaveta; we were unkind to the man!"

"What do you keep pestering me with that Cossack for?" cried Lizaveta, losing patience at last. "You stick to it like tar!"

"You are not kind, you know. . ." said Maxim, looking into his wife's face.

And for the first time since his marriage he perceived that he wife was not kind.

"I may be unkind," cried Lizaveta, tapping angrily with her spoon, "but I am not going to give away the holy Easter cake to every drunken man in the road."

"The Cossack wasn't drunk!"

"He was drunk!"

"Well, you are a fool then!"

Maxim got up from the table and began reproaching his young wife for hard-heartedness and stupidity. She, getting angry too, answered his reproaches with reproaches, burst into tears, and went away into their bedroom, declaring she would go home to her father's. This was the first matrimonial squabble that had happened in the Tortchakov's married life. He walked about the yard till the evening, picturing his wife's face, and it seemed to him now spiteful and ugly. And as though to torment him the Cossack haunted his brain, and Maxim seemed to see now his sick eyes, now his unsteady walk.

"Ah, we were unkind to the man," he muttered.

When it got dark, he was overcome by an insufferable depression such as he had never felt before. Feeling so dreary, and being angry with his wife, he got drunk, as he had sometimes done before he was married. In his drunkenness he used bad language and shouted to his wife that she had a spiteful, ugly face, and that next day he would send her packing to her father's. On the morning of Easter Monday, he drank some more to sober himself, and got drunk again.

And with that his downfall began.

His horses, cows, sheep, and hives disappeared one by one from the yard; Maxim was more and more often drunk, debts mounted up, he felt an aversion for his wife. Maxim put down all his misfortunes to the fact that he had an unkind wife, and above all, that God was angry with him on account of the sick Cossack.

Lizaveta saw their ruin, but who was to blame for it she did not understand.

Aborigines

Between nine and ten in the morning. Ivan Lyashkevsky, a lieutenant of Polish origin, who has at some time or other been wounded in the head, and now lives on his pension in a town in one of the southern provinces, is sitting in his lodgings at the open window talking to Franz Stepanitch Finks, the town architect, who has come in to see him for a minute. Both have thrust their heads out of the window, and are looking in the direction of the gate near which Lyashkevsky's landlord, a plump little native with pendulous perspiring cheeks, in full, blue trousers, is sitting on a bench with his waistcoat unbuttoned. The native is plunged in deep thought, and is absent-mindedly prodding the toe of his boot with a stick.

"Extraordinary people, I tell you," grumbled Lyashkevsky, looking angrily at the native, "here he has sat down on the bench, and so he will sit, damn the fellow, with his hands folded till evening. They do absolutely nothing. The wastrels and loafers! It would be all right, you scoundrel, if you had money lying in the bank, or had a farm of your own where others would be working for you, but here you have not a penny to your name, you eat the bread of others, you are in debt all round, and you starve your family—devil take you! You wouldn't believe me, Franz Stepanitch, sometimes it makes me so cross that I could jump out of the window and give the low fellow a good horse-whipping. Come, why don't you work? What are you sitting there for?"

The native looks indifferently at Lyashkevsky, tries to say something but cannot; sloth and the sultry heat have paralysed his conversational faculties. . . Yawning lazily, he makes the sign of the cross over his mouth, and turns his eyes up towards the sky where pigeons fly, bathing in the hot air.

"You must not be too severe in your judgments, honoured friend," sighs Finks, mopping his big bald head with his handkerchief. "Put yourself in their place: business is slack now, there's unemployment all round, a bad harvest, stagnation in trade."

"Good gracious, how you talk!" cries Lyashkevsky in indignation, angrily wrapping his dressing gown round him. "Supposing he has no job and no trade, why doesn't he work in his own home, the devil flay him! I say! Is there no work for you at home? Just look, you brute! Your steps have come to pieces, the plankway is falling into the ditch, the fence is rotten; you had better set to and mend it all, or if you don't know how, go into the kitchen and help your wife. Your wife is running out every minute to fetch water or carry out the slops. Why shouldn't you run instead, you rascal? And then you must remember, Franz Stepanitch, that he has six acres of garden, that he has pigsties and poultry houses, but it is all wasted and no use. The flower garden is overgrown with weeds and almost baked dry, while the boys play ball in the kitchen garden. Isn't he a lazy brute? I assure you, though I have only the use of an acre and a half with my lodgings, you will always find radishes, and salad, and fennel, and onions, while that blackguard buys everything at the market."

"He is a Russian, there is no doing anything with him," said Finks with a condescending smile; "it's in the Russian blood. . . They are a very lazy people! If all property were given to Germans or Poles, in a year's time you would not recognise the town."

The native in the blue trousers beckons a girl with a sieve, buys a kopeck's worth of sunflower seeds from her and begins cracking them.

"A race of curs!" says Lyashkevsky angrily. "That's their only occupation, they crack sunflower seeds and they talk politics! The devil take them!"

Staring wrathfully at the blue trousers, Lyashkevsky is gradually roused to fury, and gets so excited that he actually foams at the mouth. He speaks with a Polish accent, rapping out each syllable venomously, till at last the little bags under his eyes swell, and he abandons the Russian "scoundrels, blackguards, and rascals," and rolling his eyes, begins pouring out a shower of Polish oaths, coughing from his efforts. "Lazy dogs, race of curs. May the devil take them!"

The native hears this abuse distinctly, but, judging from the appearance of his crumpled little figure, it does not affect him. Apparently he has long ago grown as used to it as to the buzzing of the flies, and feels it superfluous to protest. At every visit Finks has to listen to a tirade on the subject of the lazy good-for-nothing aborigines, and every time exactly the same one.

"But. . . I must be going," he says, remembering that he has no time to spare. "Good-bye!"

"Where are you off to?"

"I only looked in on you for a minute. The wall of the cellar has cracked in the girls' high school, so they asked me to go round at once to look at it. I must go."

"H'm... I have told Varvara to get the samovar," says Lyashkevsky, surprised. "Stay a little, we will have some tea; then you shall go."

Finks obediently puts down his hat on the table and remains to drink tea. Over their tea Lyashkevsky maintains that the natives are hopelessly ruined, that there is only one thing to do, to take them all indiscriminately and send them under strict escort to hard labour.

"Why, upon my word," he says, getting hot, "you may ask what does that goose sitting there live upon! He lets me lodgings in his house for seven roubles a month, and he goes to name-day parties, that's all that he has to live on, the knave, may the devil take him! He has neither earnings nor an income. They are not merely sluggards and wastrels, they are swindlers too, they are continually borrowing money from the town bank, and what do they do with it? They plunge into some scheme such as sending bulls to Moscow, or building oil presses on a new system; but to send bulls to Moscow or to press oil you want to have a head on your shoulders, and these rascals have pumpkins on theirs! Of course all their schemes end in smoke... They waste their money, get into a mess, and then snap their fingers at the bank. What can you get out of them? Their houses are mortgaged over and over again, they have no other property—it's all been drunk and eaten up long ago. Nine-tenths of them are swindlers, the scoundrels! To borrow money and not return it is their rule. Thanks to them the town bank is going smash!"

"I was at Yegorov's yesterday," Finks interrupts the Pole, anxious to change the conversation, "and only fancy, I won six roubles and a half from him at picquet."

"I believe I still owe you something at picquet," Lyashkevsky recollects, "I ought to win it back. Wouldn't you like one game?"

"Perhaps just one," Finks assents. "I must make haste to the high school, you know."

Lyashkevsky and Finks sit down at the open window and begin a game of picquet. The native in the blue trousers stretches with relish, and husks of sunflower seeds fall in showers from all over him on to the ground. At that moment from the gate opposite appears another native with a long beard, wearing a crumpled yellowish-grey cotton coat. He screws up his eyes affectionately at the blue trousers and shouts:

"Good-morning, Semyon Nikolaitch, I have the honour to congratulate you on the Thursday."

"And the same to you, Kapiton Petrovitch!"

"Come to my seat! It's cool here!"

The blue trousers, with much sighing and groaning and waddling from side to side like a duck, cross the street.

"Tierce major. . ." mutters Lyashkevsky, "from the queen. . . Five and fifteen. . . The rascals are talking of politics. . . Do you hear? They have begun about England. I have six hearts."

"I have the seven spades. My point."

"Yes, it's yours. Do you hear? They are abusing Beaconsfield. They don't know, the swine, that Beaconsfield has been dead for ever so long. So I have twenty-nine. . . Your lead."

"Eight. . . nine. . . ten. . . Yes, amazing people, these Russians! Eleven. . . twelve. . . The Russian inertia is unique on the terrestrial globe."

"Thirty. . . Thirty-one. . . One ought to take a good whip, you know. Go out and give them Beaconsfield. I say, how their tongues are wagging! It's easier to babble than to work. I suppose you threw away the queen of clubs and I didn't realise it."

"Thirteen. . . Fourteen. . . It's unbearably hot! One must be made of iron to sit in such heat on a seat in the full sun! Fifteen."

The first game is followed by a second, the second by a third. . . Finks loses, and by degrees works himself up into a gambling fever and forgets all about the cracking walls of the high school cellar. As Lyashkevsky plays he keeps looking at the aborigines. He sees them, entertaining each other with conversation, go to the open gate, cross the filthy yard and sit down on a scanty patch of shade under an aspen tree. Between twelve and one o'clock the fat cook with brown legs spreads before them something like a baby's sheet with brown stains upon it, and gives them their dinner. They eat with wooden spoons, keep brushing away the flies, and go on talking.

"The devil, it is beyond everything," cries Lyashkevsky, revolted. "I am very glad I have not a gun or a revolver or I should have a shot at those cattle. I have four knaves—fourteen. . . Your point. . . It really gives me a twitching in my legs. I can't see those ruffians without being upset."

"Don't excite yourself, it is bad for you."

"But upon my word, it is enough to try the patience of a stone!"

When he has finished dinner the native in blue trousers, worn out and exhausted, staggering with laziness and repletion, crosses the street to his own house and sinks feebly on to his bench. He is struggling with drowsiness and the gnats, and is looking about him as dejectedly as though he were every minute expecting his end. His helpless air drives

Lyashkevsky out of all patience. The Pole pokes his head out of the window and shouts at him, spluttering:

"Been gorging? Ah, the old woman! The sweet darling. He has been stuffing himself, and now he doesn't know what to do with his tummy! Get out of my sight, you confounded fellow! Plague take you!"

The native looks sourly at him, and merely twiddles his fingers instead of answering. A school-boy of his acquaintance passes by him with his satchel on his back. Stopping him the native ponders a long time what to say to him, and asks:

"Well, what now?"

"Nothing."

"How, nothing?"

"Why, just nothing."

"H'm. . . And which subject is the hardest?"

"That's according." The school-boy shrugs his shoulders.

"I see—er. . . What is the Latin for tree?"

"Arbor."

"Aha. . . And so one has to know all that," sighs the blue trousers. "You have to go into it all. . . It's hard work, hard work. . . Is your dear Mamma well?"

"She is all right, thank you."

"Ah. . . Well, run along."

After losing two roubles Finks remembers the high school and is horrified.

"Holy Saints, why it's three o'clock already. How I have been staying on. Good-bye, I must run. . ."

"Have dinner with me, and then go," says Lyashkevsky. "You have plenty of time."

Finks stays, but only on condition that dinner shall last no more than ten minutes. After dining he sits for some five minutes on the sofa and thinks of the cracked wall, then resolutely lays his head on the cushion and fills the room with a shrill whistling through his nose. While he is asleep, Lyashkevsky, who does not approve of an afternoon nap, sits at the window, stares at the dozing native, and grumbles:

"Race of curs! I wonder you don't choke with laziness. No work, no intellectual or moral interests, nothing but vegetating. . . disgusting. Tfoo!"

At six o'clock Finks wakes up.

"It's too late to go to the high school now," he says, stretching. "I shall have to go to-morrow, and now. . . How about my revenge? Let's have one more game. . ."

After seeing his visitor off, between nine and ten, Lyashkevsky looks after him for some time, and says:

"Damn the fellow, staying here the whole day and doing absolutely nothing. . . Simply get their salary and do no work; the devil take them! . . . The German pig. . ."

He looks out of the window, but the native is no longer there. He has gone to bed. There is no one to grumble at, and for the first time in the day he keeps his mouth shut, but ten minutes passes and he cannot restrain the depression that overpowers him, and begins to grumble, shoving the old shabby armchair:

"You only take up room, rubbishly old thing! You ought to have been burnt long ago, but I keep forgetting to tell them to chop you up. It's a disgrace!"

And as he gets into bed he presses his hand on a spring of the mattress, frowns and says peevishly:

"The con—found—ed spring! It will cut my side all night. I will tell them to rip up the mattress to-morrow and get you out, you useless thing."

He falls asleep at midnight, and dreams that he is pouring boiling water over the natives, Finks, and the old armchair.

An Inquiry

It was midday. Voldyrev, a tall, thick-set country gentleman with a cropped head and prominent eyes, took off his overcoat, mopped his brow with his silk handkerchief, and somewhat diffidently went into the government office. There they were scratching away. . .

"Where can I make an inquiry here?" he said, addressing a porter who was bringing a trayful of glasses from the furthest recesses of the office. "I have to make an inquiry here and to take a copy of a resolution of the Council."

"That way please! To that one sitting near the window!" said the porter, indicating with the tray the furthest window. Voldyrev coughed and went towards the window; there, at a green table spotted like typhus, was sitting a young man with his hair standing up in four tufts on his head, with a long pimply nose, and a long faded uniform. He was writing, thrusting his long nose into the papers. A fly was walking about near his right nostril, and he was continually stretching out his lower lip and blowing under his nose, which gave his face an extremely care-worn expression.

"May I make an inquiry about my case here. . . of you? My name is Voldyrev. and, by the way, I have to take a copy of the resolution of the Council of the second of March."

The clerk dipped his pen in the ink and looked to see if he had got too much on it. Having satisfied himself that the pen would not make a blot, he began scribbling away. His lip was thrust out, but it was no longer necessary to blow: the fly had settled on his ear.

"Can I make an inquiry here?" Voldyrev repeated a minute later, "my name is Voldyrev, I am a landowner. . ."

"Ivan Alexeitch!" the clerk shouted into the air as though he had not observed Voldyrev, "will you tell the merchant Yalikov when he comes to sign the copy of the complaint lodged with the police! I've told him a thousand times!"

"I have come in reference to my lawsuit with the heirs of Princess Gugulin," muttered Voldyrev. "The case is well known. I earnestly beg you to attend to me."

Still failing to observe Voldyrev, the clerk caught the fly on his lip, looked at it attentively and flung it away. The country gentleman coughed and blew his nose loudly on his checked pocket handkerchief.

But this was no use either. He was still unheard. The silence lasted for two minutes. Voldyrev took a rouble note from his pocket and laid it on an open book before the clerk. The clerk wrinkled up his forehead, drew the book towards him with an anxious air and closed it.

"A little inquiry. . . I want only to find out on what grounds the heirs of Princess Gugulin. . . May I trouble you?"

The clerk, absorbed in his own thoughts, got up and, scratching his elbow, went to a cupboard for something. Returning a minute later to his table he became absorbed in the book again: another rouble note was lying upon it.

"I will trouble you for one minute only. . . I have only to make an inquiry."

The clerk did not hear, he had begun copying something.

Voldyrev frowned and looked hopelessly at the whole scribbling brotherhood.

"They write!" he thought, sighing. "They write, the devil take them entirely!"

He walked away from the table and stopped in the middle of the room, his hands hanging hopelessly at his sides. The porter, passing again with glasses, probably noticed the helpless expression of his face, for he went close up to him and asked him in a low voice:

"Well? Have you inquired?"

"I've inquired, but he wouldn't speak to me."

"You give him three roubles," whispered the porter.

"I've given him two already."

"Give him another."

Voldyrev went back to the table and laid a green note on the open book.

The clerk drew the book towards him again and began turning over the leaves, and all at once, as though by chance, lifted his eyes to Voldyrev. His nose began to shine, turned red, and wrinkled up in a grin.

"Ah. . . what do you want?" he asked.

"I want to make an inquiry in reference to my case. . . My name is Voldyrev."

"With pleasure! The Gugulin case, isn't it? Very good. What is it then exactly?"

Voldyrev explained his business.

The clerk became as lively as though he were whirled round by a hurricane. He gave the necessary information, arranged for a copy to be made, gave the petitioner a chair, and all in one instant. He even spoke about the weather and asked after the harvest. And when Voldyrev went away he accompanied him down the stairs, smiling affably and respectfully, and looking as though he were ready any minute to fall on his face before the gentleman. Voldyrev for some reason felt uncomfortable, and in obedience to some inward impulse he took a rouble out of his pocket and gave it to the clerk. And the latter kept bowing and smiling, and took the rouble like a conjuror, so that it seemed to flash through the air.

"Well, what people!" thought the country gentleman as he went out into the street, and he stopped and mopped his brow with his handkerchief.

Martyrs

Lizotchka Kudrinsky, a young married lady who had many admirers, was suddenly taken ill, and so seriously that her husband did not go to his office, and a telegram was sent to her mamma at Tver. This is how she told the story of her illness:

"I went to Lyesnoe to auntie's. I stayed there a week and then I went with all the rest to cousin Varya's. Varya's husband is a surly brute and a despot (I'd shoot a husband like that), but we had a very jolly time there. To begin with I took part in some private theatricals. It was *A Scandal in a Respectable Family*. Hrustalev acted marvellously! Between the acts I drank some cold, awfully cold, lemon squash, with the tiniest nip of brandy in it. Lemon squash with brandy in it is very much like champagne. . . I drank it and I felt nothing. Next day after the performance I rode out on horseback with that Adolf Ivanitch. It was rather damp and there was a strong wind. It was most likely then that I caught cold. Three days later I came home to see how my dear, good Vassya was getting on, and while here to get my silk dress, the one that has little flowers on it. Vassya, of course, I did not find at home. I went into the kitchen to tell Praskovya to set the samovar, and there I saw on the table some pretty little carrots and turnips like playthings. I ate one little carrot and well, a turnip too. I ate very little, but only fancy, I began having a sharp pain at once—spasms. . . spasms. . . spasms. . . ah, I am dying. Vassya runs from the office. Naturally he clutches at his hair and turns white. They run for the doctor. . . Do you understand, I am dying, dying."

The spasms began at midday, before three o'clock the doctor came, and at six Lizotchka fell asleep and slept soundly till two o'clock in the morning.

It strikes two. . . The light of the little night lamp filters scantily through the pale blue shade. Lizotchka is lying in bed, her white lace cap stands out sharply against the dark background of the red cushion. Shadows from the blue lamp-shade lie in patterns on her pale face and her round plump shoulders. Vassily Stepanovitch is sitting at her feet. The poor fellow is happy that his wife is at home at last, and at the same time he is terribly alarmed by her illness.

"Well, how do you feel, Lizotchka?" he asks in a whisper, noticing that she is awake.

"I am better," moans Lizotchka. "I don't feel the spasms now, but there is no sleeping. . . I can't get to sleep!"

"Isn't it time to change the compress, my angel?"

Lizotchka sits up slowly with the expression of a martyr and gracefully turns her head on one side. Vassily Stepanovitch with reverent awe, scarcely touching her hot body with his fingers, changes the compress. Lizotchka shrinks, laughs at the cold water which tickles her, and lies down again.

"You are getting no sleep, poor boy!" she moans.

"As though I could sleep!"

"It's my nerves, Vassya, I am a very nervous woman. The doctor has prescribed for stomach trouble, but I feel that he doesn't understand my illness. It's nerves and not the stomach, I swear that it is my nerves. There is only one thing I am afraid of, that my illness may take a bad turn."

"No, Lizotchka, no, to-morrow you will be all right!"

"Hardly likely! I am not afraid for myself. . . I don't care, indeed, I shall be glad to die, but I am sorry for you! You'll be a widower and left all alone."

Vassitchka rarely enjoys his wife's society, and has long been used to solitude, but Lizotchka's words agitate him.

"Goodness knows what you are saying, little woman! Why these gloomy thoughts?"

"Well, you will cry and grieve, and then you will get used to it. You'll even get married again."

The husband clutches his head.

"There, there, I won't!" Lizotchka soothes him, "only you ought to be prepared for anything."

"And all of a sudden I shall die," she thinks, shutting her eyes.

And Lizotchka draws a mental picture of her own death, how her mother, her husband, her cousin Varya with her husband, her relations, the admirers of her "talent" press round her death bed, as she whispers her last farewell. All are weeping. Then when she is dead they dress her, interestingly pale and dark-haired, in a pink dress (it suits her) and lay her in a very expensive coffin on gold legs, full of flowers. There is a smell of incense, the candles splutter. Her husband never leaves the coffin, while the admirers of her talent cannot take their eyes off her, and say: "As though living! She is lovely in her coffin!" The whole town is talking of the life cut short so prematurely. But now they are carrying her to the church. The bearers are Ivan Petrovitch, Adolf Ivanitch, Varya's husband, Nikolay Semyonitch, and the black-eyed student who had taught her to drink lemon squash with brandy. It's only a pity there's no music playing. After the burial service comes the leave-taking. The church is full of sobs, they bring the lid with tassels, and. . . Lizotchka is shut off from the light of day for ever, there is the sound of hammering nails. Knock, knock, knock.

Lizotchka shudders and opens her eyes.

"Vassya, are you here?" she asks. "I have such gloomy thoughts. Goodness, why am I so unlucky as not to sleep. Vassya, have pity, do tell me something!"

"What shall I tell you?"

"Something about love," Lizotchka says languidly. "Or some anecdote about Jews. . ."

Vassily Stepanovitch, ready for anything if only his wife will be cheerful and not talk about death, combs locks of hair over his ears, makes an absurd face, and goes up to Lizotchka.

"Does your vatch vant mending?" he asks.

"It does, it does," giggles Lizotchka, and hands him her gold watch from the little table. "Mend it."

Vassya takes the watch, examines the mechanism for a long time, and wriggling and shrugging, says: "She can not be mended. . . in vun veel two cogs are vanting. . ."

This is the whole performance. Lizotchka laughs and claps her hands.

"Capital," she exclaims. "Wonderful. Do you know, Vassya, it's awfully stupid of you not to take part in amateur theatricals! You have a remarkable talent! You are much better than Sysunov. There was an amateur called Sysunov who played with us in *It's My Birthday*. A first-class comic talent, only fancy: a nose as thick as a parsnip, green eyes, and he walks like a crane. . . We all roared; stay, I will show you how he walks."

Lizotchka springs out of bed and begins pacing about the floor, barefooted and without her cap.

"A very good day to you!" she says in a bass, imitating a man's voice. "Anything pretty? Anything new under the moon? Ha, ha, ha!" she laughs.

"Ha, ha, ha!" Vassya seconds her. And the young pair, roaring with laughter, forgetting the illness, chase one another about the room. The race ends in Vassya's catching his wife by her nightgown and eagerly showering kisses upon her. After one particularly passionate embrace Lizotchka suddenly remembers that she is seriously ill. . .

"What silliness!" she says, making a serious face and covering herself with the quilt. "I suppose you have forgotten that I am ill! Clever, I must say!"

"Sorry. . ." falters her husband in confusion.

"If my illness takes a bad turn it will be your fault. Not kind! not good!"

Lizotchka closes her eyes and is silent. Her former languor and expression of martyrdom return again, there is a sound of gentle moans. Vassya changes the compress, and glad that his wife is at home and not gadding off to her aunt's, sits meekly at her feet. He does not sleep all night. At ten o'clock the doctor comes.

"Well, how are we feeling?" he asks as he takes her pulse. "Have you slept?"

"Badly," Lizotchka's husband answers for her, "very badly."

The doctor walks away to the window and stares at a passing chimney-sweep.

"Doctor, may I have coffee to-day?" asks Lizotchka.

"You may."

"And may I get up?"

"You might, perhaps, but. . . you had better lie in bed another day."

"She is awfully depressed," Vassya whispers in his ear, "such gloomy thoughts, such pessimism. I am dreadfully uneasy about her."

The doctor sits down to the little table, and rubbing his forehead, prescribes bromide of potassium for Lizotchka, then makes his bow, and promising to look in again in the evening, departs. Vassya does not go to the office, but sits all day at his wife's feet.

At midday the admirers of her talent arrive in a crowd. They are agitated and alarmed, they bring masses of flowers and French novels. Lizotchka, in a snow-white cap and a light dressing jacket, lies in bed with an enigmatic look, as though she did not believe in her own recovery. The admirers of her talent see her husband, but readily forgive his presence: they and he are united by one calamity at that bedside!

At six o'clock in the evening Lizotchka falls asleep, and again sleeps till two o'clock in the morning. Vassya as before sits at her feet, struggles with drowsiness, changes her compress, plays at being a Jew, and in the morning after a second night of suffering, Liza is prinking before the looking-glass and putting on her hat.

"Wherever are you going, my dear?" asks Vassya, with an imploring look at her.

"What?" says Lizotchka in wonder, assuming a scared expression, "don't you know that there is a rehearsal to-day at Marya Lvovna's?"

After escorting her there, Vassya having nothing to do to while away his boredom, takes his portfolio and goes to the office. His head aches so violently from his sleepless nights that his left eye shuts of itself and refuses to open. . .

"What's the matter with you, my good sir?" his chief asks him. "What is it?"

Vassya waves his hand and sits down.

"Don't ask me, your Excellency," he says with a sigh. "What I have suffered in these two days, what I have suffered! Liza has been ill!"

"Good heavens," cried his chief in alarm. "Lizaveta Pavlovna, what is wrong with her?"

Vassily Stepanovitch merely throws up his hands and raises his eyes to the ceiling, as though he would say: "It's the will of Providence."

"Ah, my boy, I can sympathise with you with all my heart!" sighs his chief, rolling his eyes. "I've lost my wife, my dear, I understand. That is a loss, it is a loss! It's awful, awful! I hope Lizaveta Pavlovna is better now! What doctor is attending her?"

"Von Schterk."

"Von Schterk! But you would have been better to have called in Magnus or Semandritsky. But how very pale your face is. You are ill yourself! This is awful!"

"Yes, your Excellency, I haven't slept. What I have suffered, what I have been through!"

"And yet you came! Why you came I can't understand? One can't force oneself like that! One mustn't do oneself harm like that! Go home and stay there till you are well again! Go home, I command you! Zeal is a very fine thing in a young official, but you mustn't forget as the Romans used to say: 'mens sana in corpore sano,' that is, a healthy brain in a healthy body."

Vassya agrees, puts his papers back in his portfolio, and, taking leave of his chief, goes home to bed.

The Lion and the Sun

I n one of the towns lying on this side of the Urals a rumour was afloat that a Persian magnate, called Rahat-Helam, was staying for a few days in the town and putting up at the "Japan Hotel." This rumour made no impression whatever upon the inhabitants; a Persian had arrived, well, so be it. Only Stepan Ivanovitch Kutsyn, the mayor of the town, hearing of the arrival of the oriental gentleman from the secretary of the Town Hall, grew thoughtful and inquired:

"Where is he going?"

"To Paris or to London, I believe."

"H'm. . . Then he is a big-wig, I suppose?"

"The devil only knows."

As he went home from the Town Hall and had his dinner, the mayor sank into thought again, and this time he went on thinking till the evening. The arrival of the distinguished Persian greatly intrigued him. It seemed to him that fate itself had sent him this Rahat-Helam, and that a favourable opportunity had come at last for realising his passionate, secretly cherished dream. Kutsyn had already two medals, and the Stanislav of the third degree, the badge of the Red Cross, and the badge of the Society of Saving from Drowning, and in addition to these he had made himself a little gold gun crossed by a guitar, and this ornament, hung from a buttonhole in his uniform, looked in the distance like something special, and delightfully resembled a badge of distinction. It is well known that the more orders and medals you have the more you want—and the mayor had long been desirous of receiving the Persian order of The Lion and the Sun; he desired it passionately, madly. He knew very well that there was no need to fight, or to subscribe to an asylum, or to serve on committees to obtain this order; all that was needed was a favourable opportunity. And now it seemed to him that this opportunity had come.

At noon on the following day he put on his chain and all his badges of distinction and went to the 'Japan.' Destiny favoured him. When he entered the distinguished Persian's apartment the latter was alone and doing nothing. Rahat-Helam, an enormous Asiatic, with a long nose like the beak of a snipe, with prominent eyes, and with a fez on his head, was sitting on the floor rummaging in his portmanteau.

"I beg you to excuse my disturbing you," began Kutsyn, smiling. "I have the honour to introduce myself, the hereditary, honourable citizen and cavalier, Stepan Ivanovitch Kutsyn, mayor of this town. I regard it as my duty to honour, in the person of your Highness, so to say, the representative of a friendly and neighbourly state."

The Persian turned and muttered something in very bad French, that sounded like tapping a board with a piece of wood.

"The frontiers of Persia"—Kutsyn continued the greeting he had previously learned by heart—"are in close contact with the borders of our spacious fatherland, and therefore mutual sympathies impel me, so to speak, to express my solidarity with you."

The illustrious Persian got up and again muttered something in a wooden tongue. Kutsyn, who knew no foreign language, shook his head to show that he did not understand.

"Well, how am I to talk to him?" he thought. "It would be a good thing to send for an interpreter at once, but it is a delicate matter, I can't talk before witnesses. The interpreter would be chattering all over the town afterwards."

And Kutsyn tried to recall the foreign words he had picked up from the newspapers.

"I am the mayor of the town," he muttered. "That is the *lord mayor. . . municipalais. . .* Vwee? Kompreney?"

He wanted to express his social position in words or in gesture, and did not know how. A picture hanging on the wall with an inscription in large letters, "The Town of Venice," helped him out of his difficulties. He pointed with his finger at the town, then at his own head, and in that way obtained, as he imagined, the phrase: "I am the head of the town." The Persian did not understand, but he gave a smile, and said:

"Goot, monsieur. . . goot. . ." Half-an-hour later the mayor was slapping the Persian, first on the knee and then on the shoulder, and saying:

"Kompreney? Vwee? As *lord mayor* and *municipalais* I suggest that you should take a little *promenage. . . kompreney? Promenage.* "

Kutsyn pointed at Venice, and with two fingers represented walking legs. Rahat-Helam who kept his eyes fixed on his medals, and was apparently guessing that this was the most important person in the town, understood the word *promenage* and grinned politely. Then they both put on their coats and went out of the room. Downstairs near the door leading to the restaurant of the 'Japan,' Kutsyn reflected that it would not be amiss to entertain the Persian. He stopped and indicating the tables, said:

"By Russian custom it wouldn't be amiss. . . *puree, entrekot*, champagne and so on, kompreney."

The illustrious visitor understood, and a little later they were both sitting in the very best room of the restaurant, eating, and drinking champagne.

"Let us drink to the prosperity of Persia!" said Kutsyn. "We Russians love the Persians. Though we are of another faith, yet there are common interests, mutual, so to say, sympathies. . . progress. . . Asiatic markets. . . The campaigns of peace so to say. . ."

The illustrious Persian ate and drank with an excellent appetite, he stuck his fork into a slice of smoked sturgeon, and wagging his head, enthusiastically said: "*Goot, bien.*"

"You like it?" said the mayor delighted. "*Bien*, that's capital." And turning to the waiter he said: "Luka, my lad, see that two pieces of smoked sturgeon, the best you have, are sent up to his Highness's room!"

Then the mayor and the Persian magnate went to look at the menagerie. The townspeople saw their Stepan Ivanovitch, flushed with champagne, gay and very well pleased, leading the Persian about the principal streets and the bazaar, showing him the points of interest of the town, and even taking him to the fire tower.

Among other things the townspeople saw him stop near some stone gates with lions on it, and point out to the Persian first the lion, then the sun overhead, and then his own breast; then again he pointed to the lion and to the sun while the Persian nodded his head as though in sign of assent, and smiling showed his white teeth. In the evening they were sitting in the London Hotel listening to the harp-players, and where they spent the night is not known.

Next day the mayor was at the Town Hall in the morning; the officials there apparently already knew something and were making their conjectures, for the secretary went up to him and said with an ironical smile:

"It is the custom of the Persians when an illustrious visitor comes to visit you, you must slaughter a sheep with your own hands."

And a little later an envelope that had come by post was handed to him. The mayor tore it open and saw a caricature in it. It was a drawing of Rahat-Helam with the mayor on his knees before him, stretching out his hands and saying:

> *"To prove our Russian friendship*
> *For Persia's mighty realm,*
> *And show respect for you, her envoy,*
> *Myself I'd slaughter like a lamb,*
> *But, pardon me, for I'm a—donkey!"*

The mayor was conscious of an unpleasant feeling like a gnawing in the pit of the stomach, but not for long. By midday he was again with the illustrious Persian, again he was regaling him and showing him the points of interest in the town. Again he led him to the stone gates, and again pointed to the lion, to the sun and to his own breast. They dined at the 'Japan'; after dinner, with cigars in their teeth, both, flushed and blissful, again mounted the fire tower, and the mayor, evidently wishing to entertain the visitor with an unusual spectacle, shouted from the top to a sentry walking below:

"Sound the alarm!"

But the alarm was not sounded as the firemen were at the baths at the moment.

They supped at the 'London' and, after supper, the Persian departed. When he saw him off, Stepan Ivanovitch kissed him three times after the Russian fashion, and even grew tearful. And when the train started, he shouted:

"Give our greeting to Persia! Tell her that we love her!"

A year and four months had passed. There was a bitter frost, thirty-five degrees, and a piercing wind was blowing. Stepan Ivanovitch was walking along the street with his fur coat thrown open over his chest, and he was annoyed that he met no one to see the Lion and the Sun upon his breast. He walked about like this till evening with his fur coat open, was chilled to the bone, and at night tossed from side to side and could not get to sleep.

He felt heavy at heart.

There was a burning sensation inside him, and his heart throbbed uneasily; he had a longing now to get a Serbian order. It was a painful, passionate longing.

ANTON CHEKHOV

A Daughter of Albion

A Fine carriage with rubber tyres, a fat coachman, and velvet on the seats, rolled up to the house of a landowner called Gryabov. Fyodor Andreitch Otsov, the district Marshal of Nobility, jumped out of the carriage. A drowsy footman met him in the hall.

"Are the family at home?" asked the Marshal.

"No, sir. The mistress and the children are gone out paying visits, while the master and mademoiselle are catching fish. Fishing all the morning, sir."

Otsov stood a little, thought a little, and then went to the river to look for Gryabov. Going down to the river he found him a mile and a half from the house. Looking down from the steep bank and catching sight of Gryabov, Otsov gushed with laughter. . . Gryabov, a large stout man, with a very big head, was sitting on the sand, angling, with his legs tucked under him like a Turk. His hat was on the back of his head and his cravat had slipped on one side. Beside him stood a tall thin Englishwoman, with prominent eyes like a crab's, and a big bird-like nose more like a hook than a nose. She was dressed in a white muslin gown through which her scraggy yellow shoulders were very distinctly apparent. On her gold belt hung a little gold watch. She too was angling. The stillness of the grave reigned about them both. Both were motionless, as the river upon which their floats were swimming.

"A desperate passion, but deadly dull!" laughed Otsov. "Good-day, Ivan Kuzmitch."

"Ah. . . is that you?" asked Gryabov, not taking his eyes off the water. "Have you come?"

"As you see. . . And you are still taken up with your crazy nonsense! Not given it up yet?"

"The devil's in it. . . I begin in the morning and fish all day. . . The fishing is not up to much to-day. I've caught nothing and this dummy hasn't either. We sit on and on and not a devil of a fish! I could scream!"

"Well, chuck it up then. Let's go and have some vodka!"

"Wait a little, maybe we shall catch something. Towards evening the fish bite better. . . I've been sitting here, my boy, ever since the morning! I can't tell you how fearfully boring it is. It was the devil drove me to take to this fishing! I know that it is rotten idiocy for me to sit here. I sit here like some scoundrel, like a convict, and I stare at the water like a fool. I ought to go to the haymaking, but here I sit catching fish. Yesterday His Holiness held a service at Haponyevo, but I didn't go. I spent the day here with this. . . with this she-devil."

"But. . . have you taken leave of your senses?" asked Otsov, glancing in embarrassment at the Englishwoman. "Using such language before a lady and she. . ."

"Oh, confound her, it doesn't matter, she doesn't understand a syllable of Russian, whether you praise her or blame her, it is all the same to her! Just look at her nose! Her nose alone is enough to make one faint. We sit here for whole days together and not a single word! She stands like a stuffed image and rolls the whites of her eyes at the water."

The Englishwoman gave a yawn, put a new worm on, and dropped the hook into the water.

"I wonder at her not a little," Gryabov went on, "the great stupid has been living in Russia for ten years and not a word of Russian! . . . Any little aristocrat among us goes to them and learns to babble away in their lingo, while they. . . there's no making them out. Just look at her nose, do look at her nose!"

"Come, drop it. . . it's uncomfortable. Why attack a woman?"

"She's not a woman, but a maiden lady. . . I bet she's dreaming of suitors. The ugly doll. And she smells of something decaying. . . I've got a loathing for her, my boy! I can't look at her with indifference. When she turns her ugly eyes on me it sends a twinge all through me as though I had knocked my elbow on the parapet. She likes fishing too. Watch her: she fishes as though it were a holy rite! She looks upon everything with disdain. . . She stands there, the wretch, and is conscious that she is a human being, and that therefore she is the monarch of nature. And do you know what her name is? Wilka Charlesovna Fyce! Tfoo! There is no getting it out!"

The Englishwoman, hearing her name, deliberately turned her nose in Gryabov's direction and scanned him with a disdainful glance; she raised her eyes from Gryabov to Otsov and steeped him in disdain. And all this in silence, with dignity and deliberation.

"Did you see?" said Gryabov chuckling. "As though to say 'take that.' Ah, you monster! It's only for the children's sake that I keep that triton. If it weren't for the children, I wouldn't let her come within ten miles of my estate. . . She has got a nose like a hawk's. . . and her figure! That doll makes me think of a long nail, so I could take her, and knock her into the ground, you know. Stay, I believe I have got a bite. . ."

Gryabov jumped up and raised his rod. The line drew taut. . . Gryabov tugged again, but could not pull out the hook.

"It has caught," he said, frowning, "on a stone I expect. . . damnation take it. . ."

There was a look of distress on Gryabov's face. Sighing, moving uneasily, and muttering oaths, he began tugging at the line.

"What a pity; I shall have to go into the water."

"Oh, chuck it!"

"I can't. . . There's always good fishing in the evening. . . What a nuisance. Lord, forgive us, I shall have to wade into the water, I must! And if only you knew, I have no inclination to undress. I shall have to get rid of the Englishwoman. . . It's awkward to undress before her. After all, she is a lady, you know!"

Gryabov flung off his hat, and his cravat.

"Meess. . . er, er. . ." he said, addressing the Englishwoman, "Meess Fyce, je voo pree. . . ? Well, what am I to say to her? How am I to tell you so that you can understand? I say. . . over there! Go away over there! Do you hear?"

Miss Fyce enveloped Gryabov in disdain, and uttered a nasal sound.

"What? Don't you understand? Go away from here, I tell you! I must undress, you devil's doll! Go over there! Over there!"

Gryabov pulled the lady by her sleeve, pointed her towards the bushes, and made as though he would sit down, as much as to say: Go behind the bushes and hide yourself there. . . The Englishwoman, moving her eyebrows vigorously, uttered rapidly a long sentence in English. The gentlemen gushed with laughter.

"It's the first time in my life I've heard her voice. There's no denying, it is a voice! She does not understand! Well, what am I to do with her?"

"Chuck it, let's go and have a drink of vodka!"

"I can't. Now's the time to fish, the evening. . . It's evening. . . Come, what would you have me do? It is a nuisance! I shall have to undress before her. . ."

Gryabov flung off his coat and his waistcoat and sat on the sand to take off his boots.

"I say, Ivan Kuzmitch," said the marshal, chuckling behind his hand. "It's really outrageous, an insult."

"Nobody asks her not to understand! It's a lesson for these foreigners!"

Gryabov took off his boots and his trousers, flung off his undergarments and remained in the costume of Adam. Otsov held his sides, he turned crimson both from laughter and embarrassment. The Englishwoman twitched her brows and blinked... A haughty, disdainful smile passed over her yellow face.

"I must cool off," said Gryabov, slapping himself on the ribs. "Tell me if you please, Fyodor Andreitch, why I have a rash on my chest every summer."

"Oh, do get into the water quickly or cover yourself with something, you beast."

"And if only she were confused, the nasty thing," said Gryabov, crossing himself as he waded into the water. "Brrrr... the water's cold... Look how she moves her eyebrows! She doesn't go away... she is far above the crowd! He, he, he... and she doesn't reckon us as human beings."

Wading knee deep in the water and drawing his huge figure up to its full height, he gave a wink and said:

"This isn't England, you see!"

Miss Fyce coolly put on another worm, gave a yawn, and dropped the hook in. Otsov turned away, Gryabov released his hook, ducked into the water and, spluttering, waded out. Two minutes later he was sitting on the sand and angling as before.

CHORISTERS

The Justice of the Peace, who had received a letter from Petersburg, had set the news going that the owner of Yefremovo, Count Vladimir Ivanovitch, would soon be arriving. When he would arrive—there was no saying.

"Like a thief in the night," said Father Kuzma, a grey-headed little priest in a lilac cassock. "And when he does come the place will be crowded with the nobility and other high gentry. All the neighbours will flock here. Mind now, do your best, Alexey Alexeitch. . . I beg you most earnestly."

"You need not trouble about me," said Alexey Alexeitch, frowning. "I know my business. If only my enemy intones the litany in the right key. He may. . . out of sheer spite. . ."

"There, there. . . I'll persuade the deacon. . . I'll persuade him."

Alexey Alexeitch was the sacristan of the Yefremovo church. He also taught the schoolboys church and secular singing, for which he received sixty roubles a year from the revenues of the Count's estate. The schoolboys were bound to sing in church in return for their teaching. Alexey Alexeitch was a tall, thick-set man of dignified deportment, with a fat, clean-shaven face that reminded one of a cow's udder. His imposing figure and double chin made him look like a man occupying an important position in the secular hierarchy rather than a sacristan. It was strange to see him, so dignified and imposing, flop to the ground before the bishop and, on one occasion, after too loud a squabble with the deacon Yevlampy Avdiessov, remain on his knees for two hours by order of the head priest of the district. Grandeur was more in keeping with his figure than humiliation.

On account of the rumours of the Count's approaching visit he had a choir practice every day, morning and evening. The choir practice was held at the school. It did not interfere much with the school work. During the practice the schoolmaster, Sergey Makaritch, set the children writing copies while he joined the tenors as an amateur.

This is how the choir practice was conducted. Alexey Alexeitch would come into the school-room, slamming the door and blowing his nose. The trebles and altos extricated themselves noisily from the school-tables. The tenors and basses, who had been waiting for some time in the yard, came in, tramping like horses. They all took their places. Alexey Alexeitch drew himself up, made a sign to enforce silence, and struck a note with the tuning fork.

"To-to-li-to-tom. . . Do-mi-sol-do!"

"Adagio, adagio. . . Once more."

After the "Amen" there followed "Lord have mercy upon us" from the Great Litany. All this had been learned long ago, sung a thousand times and thoroughly digested, and it was gone through simply as a formality. It was sung indolently, unconsciously. Alexey Alexeitch waved his arms calmly and chimed in now in a tenor, now in a bass voice. It was all slow, there was nothing interesting. . . But before the "Cherubim" hymn the whole choir suddenly began blowing their noses, coughing and zealously turning the pages of their music. The sacristan turned his back on the choir and with a mysterious expression on his face began tuning his violin. The preparations lasted a couple of minutes.

"Take your places. Look at your music carefully. . . Basses, don't overdo it. . . rather softly."

Bortnyansky's "Cherubim" hymn, No. 7, was selected. At a given signal silence prevailed. All eyes were fastened on the music, the trebles opened their mouths. Alexey Alexeitch softly lowered his arm.

"Piano. . . piano. . . You see 'piano' is written there. . . More lightly, more lightly."

When they had to sing "piano" an expression of benevolence and amiability overspread Alexey Alexeitch's face, as though he was dreaming of a dainty morsel.

"Forte. . . forte! Hold it!"

And when they had to sing "forte" the sacristan's fat face expressed alarm and even horror.

The "Cherubim" hymn was sung well, so well that the school-children abandoned their copies and fell to watching the movements of Alexey Alexeitch. People stood under the windows. The schoolwatchman, Vassily, came in wearing an apron and carrying a dinner-knife in his hand and stood listening. Father Kuzma, with an anxious face appeared suddenly as though he had sprung from out of the earth. . . After 'Let us lay aside all earthly cares' Alexey Alexeitch wiped the sweat off his brow and went up to Father Kuzma in excitement.

"It puzzles me, Father Kuzma," he said, shrugging his shoulders, "why is it that the Russian people have no understanding? It puzzles me, may the Lord chastise me! Such an uncultured people that you really cannot tell whether they have a windpipe in their throats or some other sort of internal arrangement. Were you choking, or what?" he asked, addressing the bass Gennady Semitchov, the innkeeper's brother.

"Why?"

"What is your voice like? It rattles like a saucepan. I bet you were boozing yesterday! That's what it is! Your breath smells like a tavern. . . E-ech! You are a clodhopper, brother! You are a lout! How can you be a chorister if you keep company with peasants in the tavern? Ech, you are an ass, brother!"

"It's a sin, it's a sin, brother," muttered Father Kuzma. "God sees everything. . . through and through. . ."

"That's why you have no idea of singing—because you care more for vodka than for godliness, you fool."

"Don't work yourself up," said Father Kuzma. "Don't be cross. . . I will persuade him."

Father Kuzma went up to Gennady Semitchov and began "persuading" him: "What do you do it for? Try and put your mind to it. A man who sings ought to restrain himself, because his throat is. . . er . . tender."

Gennady scratched his neck and looked sideways towards the window as though the words did not apply to him.

After the "Cherubim" hymn they sang the Creed, then "It is meet and right"; they sang smoothly and with feeling, and so right on to "Our Father."

"To my mind, Father Kuzma," said the sacristan, "the old 'Our Father' is better than the modern. That's what we ought to sing before the Count."

"No, no. . . Sing the modern one. For the Count hears nothing but modern music when he goes to Mass in Petersburg or Moscow. . . In the churches there, I imagine. . . there's very different sort of music there, brother!"

After "Our Father" there was again a great blowing of noses, coughing and turning over of pages. The most difficult part of the performance came next: the "concert." Alexey Alexeitch was practising two pieces, "Who is the God of glory" and "Universal Praise." Whichever the choir learned best would be sung before the Count. During the "concert" the sacristan rose to a pitch of enthusiasm. The expression of benevolence was continually alternating with one of alarm.

"Forte!" he muttered. "Andante! let yourselves go! Sing, you image! Tenors, you don't bring it off! To-to-ti-to-tom. . . Sol. . . si. . . sol, I tell you, you blockhead! Glory! Basses, glo. . . o. . . ry."

His bow travelled over the heads and shoulders of the erring trebles and altos. His left hand was continually pulling the ears of the young singers. On one occasion, carried away by his feelings he flipped the bass Gennady under the chin with his bent thumb. But the choristers were not moved to tears or to anger at his blows: they realised the full gravity of their task.

After the "concert" came a minute of silence. Alexey Alexeitch, red, perspiring and exhausted, sat down on the window-sill, and turned upon the company lustreless, wearied, but triumphant eyes. In the listening crowd he observed to his immense annoyance the deacon Avdiessov. The deacon, a tall thick-set man with a red pock-marked face, and straw in his hair, stood leaning against the stove and grinning contemptuously.

"That's right, sing away! Perform your music!" he muttered in a deep bass. "Much the Count will care for your singing! He doesn't care whether you sing with music or without. . . For he is an atheist."

Father Kuzma looked round in a scared way and twiddled his fingers.

"Come, come," he muttered. "Hush, deacon, I beg."

After the "concert" they sang "May our lips be filled with praise," and the choir practice was over. The choir broke up to reassemble in the evening for another practice. And so it went on every day.

One month passed and then a second. . . The steward, too, had by then received a notice that the Count would soon be coming. At last the dusty sun-blinds were taken off the windows of the big house, and Yefremovo heard the strains of the broken-down, out-of-tune piano. Father Kuzma was pining, though he could not himself have said why, or whether it was from delight or alarm. . . The deacon went about grinning.

The following Saturday evening Father Kuzma went to the sacristan's lodgings. His face was pale, his shoulders drooped, the lilac of his cassock looked faded.

"I have just been at his Excellency's," he said to the sacristan, stammering. "He is a cultivated gentleman with refined ideas. But. . . er. . . it's mortifying, brother. . . 'At what o'clock, your Excellency, do you desire us to ring for Mass to-morrow?' And he said: 'As you think best. Only, couldn't it be as short and quick as possible without a choir.' Without a choir! Er. . . do you understand, without, without a choir. . ."

Alexey Alexeitch turned crimson. He would rather have spent two hours on his knees again than have heard those words! He did not sleep all night. He was not so much mortified at the waste of his labours as at the fact that the deacon would give him no peace now with his jeers. The deacon was delighted at his discomfiture. Next day all through the service he was casting disdainful glances towards the choir where Alexey Alexeitch was booming responses in solitude. When he passed by the choir with the censer he muttered:

"Perform your music! Do your utmost! The Count will give a ten-rouble note to the choir!"

After the service the sacristan went home, crushed and ill with mortification. At the gate he was overtaken by the red-faced deacon.

"Stop a minute, Alyosha!" said the deacon. "Stop a minute, silly, don't be cross! You are not the only one, I am in for it too! Immediately after the Mass Father Kuzma went up to the Count and asked: 'And what did you think of the deacon's voice, your Excellency. He has a deep bass, hasn't he?' And the Count—do you know what he answered by way of compliment? 'Anyone can bawl,' he said. 'A man's voice is not as important as his brains.' A learned gentleman from Petersburg! An atheist is an atheist, and that's all about it! Come, brother in misfortune, let us go and have a drop to drown our troubles!"

And the enemies went out of the gate arm-in-arm.

Nerves

Dmitri Osipovitch Vaxin, the architect, returned from town to his holiday cottage greatly impressed by the spiritualistic séance at which he had been present. As he undressed and got into his solitary bed (Madame Vaxin had gone to an all-night service) he could not help remembering all he had seen and heard. It had not, properly speaking, been a séance at all, but the whole evening had been spent in terrifying conversation. A young lady had begun it by talking, apropos of nothing, about thought-reading. From thought-reading they had passed imperceptibly to spirits, and from spirits to ghosts, from ghosts to people buried alive. . . A gentleman had read a horrible story of a corpse turning round in the coffin. Vaxin himself had asked for a saucer and shown the young ladies how to converse with spirits. He had called up among others the spirit of his deceased uncle, Klavdy Mironitch, and had mentally asked him:

"Has not the time come for me to transfer the ownership of our house to my wife?"

To which his uncle's spirit had replied:

"All things are good in their season."

"There is a great deal in nature that is mysterious and. . . terrible. . ." thought Vaxin, as he got into bed. "It's not the dead but the unknown that's so horrible."

It struck one o'clock. Vaxin turned over on the other side and peeped out from beneath the bedclothes at the blue light of the lamp burning before the holy ikon. The flame flickered and cast a faint light on the ikon-stand and the big portrait of Uncle Klavdy that hung facing his bed.

"And what if the ghost of Uncle Klavdy should appear this minute?" flashed through Vaxin's mind. "But, of course, that's impossible."

Ghosts are, we all know, a superstition, the offspring of undeveloped intelligence, but Vaxin, nevertheless, pulled the bed-clothes over his head, and shut his eyes very tight. The corpse that turned round in its coffin came back to his mind, and the figures of his deceased mother-in-law, of a colleague who had hanged himself, and of a girl who had drowned herself, rose before his imagination. . . Vaxin began trying to dispel these gloomy ideas, but the more he tried to drive them away the more haunting the figures and fearful fancies became. He began to feel frightened.

"Hang it all!" he thought. "Here I am afraid in the dark like a child! Idiotic!"

Tick. . . tick. . . tick. . . he heard the clock in the next room. The church-bell chimed the hour in the churchyard close by. The bell tolled slowly, depressingly, mournfully. . . A cold chill ran down Vaxin's neck and spine. He fancied he heard someone breathing heavily over his head, as though Uncle Klavdy had stepped out of his frame and was bending over his nephew. . . Vaxin felt unbearably frightened. He clenched his teeth and held his breath in terror.

At last, when a cockchafer flew in at the open window and began buzzing over his bed, he could bear it no longer and gave a violent tug at the bellrope.

"Dmitri Osipitch, *was wollen Sie?*" he heard the voice of the German governess at his door a moment later.

"Ah, it's you, Rosalia Karlovna!" Vaxin cried, delighted. "Why do you trouble? Gavrila might just. . ."

"Yourself Gavrila to the town sent. And Glafira is somewhere all the evening gone. . . There's nobody in the house. . . *Was wollen Sie doch?*"

"Well, what I wanted. . . it's. . . but, please, come in. . . you needn't mind! . . . it's dark."

Rosalia Karlovna, a stout red-cheeked person, came in to the bedroom and stood in an expectant attitude at the door.

"Sit down, please. . . you see, it's like this. . . What on earth am I to ask her for?" he wondered, stealing a glance at Uncle Klavdy's portrait and feeling his soul gradually returning to tranquility.

"What I really wanted to ask you was. . . Oh, when the man goes to town, don't forget to tell him to. . . er. . . er. . . to get some cigarette-papers. . . But do, please sit down."

"Cigarette-papers? good. . . *Was wollen Sie noch?*"

"*Ich will*. . . there's nothing I will, but. . . But do sit down! I shall think of something else in a minute."

"It is shocking for a maiden in a man's room to remain. . . Mr. Vaxin, you are, I see, a naughty man. . . I understand. . . To order cigarette-papers one does not a person wake. . . I understand you. . ."

Rosalia Karlovna turned and went out of the room.

Somewhat reassured by his conversation with her and ashamed of his cowardice, Vaxin pulled the bedclothes over his head and shut his eyes. For about ten minutes he felt fairly comfortable, then the same nonsense came creeping back into his mind. . . He swore to himself, felt for the matches, and without opening his eyes lighted a candle.

But even the light was no use. To Vaxin's excited imagination it seemed as though someone were peeping round the corner and that his uncle's eyes were moving.

"I'll ring her up again. . . damn the woman!" he decided. "I'll tell her I'm unwell and ask for some drops."

Vaxin rang. There was no response. He rang again, and as though answering his ring, he heard the church-bell toll the hour.

Overcome with terror, cold all over, he jumped out of bed, ran headlong out of his bedroom, and making the sign of the cross and cursing himself for his cowardice, he fled barefoot in his night-shirt to the governess's room.

"Rosalia Karlovna!" he began in a shaking voice as he knocked at her door, "Rosalia Karlovna! . . . Are you asleep? . . . I feel. . . so. . . er. . . er. . . unwell. . . Drops! . . ."

There was no answer. Silence reigned.

"I beg you. . . do you understand? I beg you! Why this squeamishness, I can't understand. . . especially when a man. . . is ill. . . How absurdly *zierlich manierlich* you are really. . . at your age. . ."

"I to your wife shall tell. . . Will not leave an honest maiden in peace. . . When I was at Baron Anzig's, and the baron try to come to me for matches, I understand at once what his matches mean and tell to the baroness. . . I am an honest maiden."

"Hang your honesty! I am ill I tell you. . . and asking you for drops. Do you understand? I'm ill!"

"Your wife is an honest, good woman, and you ought her to love! *Ja!* She is noble! . . . I will not be her foe!"

"You are a fool! simply a fool! Do you understand, a fool?"

Vaxin leaned against the door-post, folded his arms and waited for his panic to pass off. To return to his room where the lamp flickered and his uncle stared at him from his frame was more than he could face, and to stand at the governess's door in nothing but his night-shirt was inconvenient from every point of view. What could he do?

It struck two o'clock and his terror had not left him. There was no light in the passage and something dark seemed to be peeping out from every corner. Vaxin turned so as to face the door-post, but at that instant it seemed as though somebody tweaked his night-shirt from behind and touched him on the shoulder.

ANTON CHEKHOV

"Damnation! . . . Rosalia Karlovna!"

No answer. Vaxin hesitatingly opened the door and peeped into the room. The virtuous German was sweetly slumbering. The tiny flame of a night-light threw her solid buxom person into relief. Vaxin stepped into the room and sat down on a wickerwork trunk near the door. He felt better in the presence of a living creature, even though that creature was asleep.

"Let the German idiot sleep," he thought, "I'll sit here, and when it gets light I'll go back. . . It's daylight early now."

Vaxin curled up on the trunk and put his arm under his head to await the coming of dawn.

"What a thing it is to have nerves!" he reflected. "An educated, intelligent man! . . . Hang it all! . . . It's a perfect disgrace!"

As he listened to the gentle, even breathing of Rosalia Karlovna, he soon recovered himself completely.

At six o'clock, Vaxin's wife returned from the all-night service, and not finding her husband in their bedroom, went to the governess to ask her for some change for the cabman.

On entering the German's room, a strange sight met her eyes.

On the bed lay stretched Rosalia Karlovna fast asleep, and a couple of yards from her was her husband curled up on the trunk sleeping the sleep of the just and snoring loudly.

What she said to her husband, and how he looked when he woke, I leave to others to describe. It is beyond my powers.

A Work of Art

S asha Smirnov, the only son of his mother, holding under his arm, something wrapped up in No. 223 of the *Financial News*, assumed a sentimental expression, and went into Dr. Koshelkov's consulting-room.

"Ah, dear lad!" was how the doctor greeted him. "Well! how are we feeling? What good news have you for me?"

Sasha blinked, laid his hand on his heart and said in an agitated voice: "Mamma sends her greetings to you, Ivan Nikolaevitch, and told me to thank you. . . I am the only son of my mother and you have saved my life. . . you have brought me through a dangerous illness and. . . we do not know how to thank you."

"Nonsense, lad!" said the doctor, highly delighted. "I only did what anyone else would have done in my place."

"I am the only son of my mother. . . we are poor people and cannot of course repay you, and we are quite ashamed, doctor, although, however, mamma and I. . . the only son of my mother, earnestly beg you to accept in token of our gratitude. . . this object, which. . . An object of great value, an antique bronze. . . A rare work of art."

"You shouldn't!" said the doctor, frowning. "What's this for!"

"No, please do not refuse," Sasha went on muttering as he unpacked the parcel. "You will wound mamma and me by refusing. . . It's a fine thing. . . an antique bronze. . . It was left us by my deceased father and we have kept it as a precious souvenir. My father used to buy antique bronzes and sell them to connoisseurs. . . Mamma and I keep on the business now."

Sasha undid the object and put it solemnly on the table. It was a not very tall candelabra of old bronze and artistic workmanship. It consisted of a group: on the pedestal stood two female figures in the costume of Eve and in attitudes for the description of which I have neither the courage nor the fitting temperament. The figures were smiling coquettishly and altogether looked as though, had it not been for the necessity of supporting the candlestick, they would have skipped off the pedestal and have indulged in an orgy such as is improper for the reader even to imagine.

Looking at the present, the doctor slowly scratched behind his ear, cleared his throat and blew his nose irresolutely.

"Yes, it certainly is a fine thing," he muttered, "but. . . how shall I express it? . . . it's. . . h'm. . . it's not quite for family reading. It's not simply decolleté but beyond anything, dash it all. . ."

"How do you mean?"

"The serpent-tempter himself could not have invented anything worse. . . Why, to put such a phantasmagoria on the table would be defiling the whole flat."

"What a strange way of looking at art, doctor!" said Sasha, offended. "Why, it is an artistic thing, look at it! There is so much beauty and elegance that it fills one's soul with a feeling of reverence and brings a lump into one's throat! When one sees anything so beautiful one forgets everything earthly. . . Only look, how much movement, what an atmosphere, what expression!"

"I understand all that very well, my dear boy," the doctor interposed, "but you know I am a family man, my children run in here, ladies come in."

"Of course if you look at it from the point of view of the crowd," said Sasha, "then this exquisitely artistic work may appear in a certain light. . . But, doctor, rise superior to the crowd, especially as you will wound mamma and me by refusing it. I am the only son of my mother, you have saved my life. . . We are giving you the thing most precious to us and. . . and I only regret that I have not the pair to present to you. . ."

"Thank you, my dear fellow, I am very grateful. . . Give my respects to your mother but really consider, my children run in here, ladies come. . . However, let it remain! I see there's no arguing with you."

"And there is nothing to argue about," said Sasha, relieved. "Put the candlestick here, by this vase. What a pity we have not the pair to it! It is a pity! Well, good-bye, doctor."

After Sasha's departure the doctor looked for a long time at the candelabra, scratched behind his ear and meditated.

"It's a superb thing, there's no denying it," he thought, "and it would be a pity to throw it away. . . But it's impossible for me to keep it. . . H'm! . . . Here's a problem! To whom can I make a present of it, or to what charity can I give it?"

After long meditation he thought of his good friend, the lawyer Uhov, to whom he was indebted for the management of legal business.

"Excellent," the doctor decided, "it would be awkward for him as a friend to take money from me, and it will be very suitable for me to present him with this. I will take him the devilish thing! Luckily he is a bachelor and easy-going."

Without further procrastination the doctor put on his hat and coat, took the candelabra and went off to Uhov's.

"How are you, friend!" he said, finding the lawyer at home. "I've come to see you. . . to thank you for your efforts. . . You won't take money so you must at least accept this thing here. . . See, my dear fellow. . . The thing is magnificent!"

On seeing the bronze the lawyer was moved to indescribable delight.

"What a specimen!" he chuckled. "Ah, deuce take it, to think of them imagining such a thing, the devils! Exquisite! Ravishing! Where did you get hold of such a delightful thing?"

After pouring out his ecstasies the lawyer looked timidly towards the door and said: "Only you must carry off your present, my boy. . . I can't take it. . ."

"Why?" cried the doctor, disconcerted.

"Why. . . because my mother is here at times, my clients. . . besides I should be ashamed for my servants to see it."

"Nonsense! Nonsense! Don't you dare to refuse!" said the doctor, gesticulating. "It's piggish of you! It's a work of art! . . . What movement. . . what expression! I won't even talk of it! You will offend me!"

"If one could plaster it over or stick on fig-leaves. . ."

But the doctor gesticulated more violently than before, and dashing out of the flat went home, glad that he had succeeded in getting the present off his hands.

When he had gone away the lawyer examined the candelabra, fingered it all over, and then, like the doctor, racked his brains over the question what to do with the present.

"It's a fine thing," he mused, "and it would be a pity to throw it away and improper to keep it. The very best thing would be to make a present of it to someone. . . I know what! I'll take it this evening to Shashkin, the comedian. The rascal is fond of such things, and by the way it is his benefit tonight."

No sooner said than done. In the evening the candelabra, carefully wrapped up, was duly carried to Shashkin's. The whole evening the comic actor's dressing-room was besieged by men coming to admire the present; the dressing-room was filled with the hum of enthusiasm and laughter like the neighing of horses. If one of the actresses approached the door and asked: "May I come in?" the comedian's husky voice was heard at once: "No, no, my dear, I am not dressed!"

After the performance the comedian shrugged his shoulders, flung up his hands and said: "Well what am I to do with the horrid thing? Why, I live in a private flat! Actresses come and see me! It's not a photograph that you can put in a drawer!"

"You had better sell it, sir," the hairdresser who was disrobing the actor advised him. "There's an old woman living about here who buys antique bronzes. Go and enquire for Madame Smirnov. . . everyone knows her."

The actor followed his advice. . . Two days later the doctor was sitting in his consulting-room, and with his finger to his brow was meditating on the acids of the bile. All at once the door opened and Sasha Smirnov flew into the room. He was smiling, beaming, and his whole figure was radiant with happiness. In his hands he held something wrapped up in newspaper.

"Doctor!" he began breathlessly, "imagine my delight! Happily for you we have succeeded in picking up the pair to your candelabra! Mamma is so happy. . . I am the only son of my mother, you saved my life. . ."

And Sasha, all of a tremor with gratitude, set the candelabra before the doctor. The doctor opened his mouth, tried to say something, but said nothing: he could not speak.

A JOKE

It was a bright winter midday. . . There was a sharp snapping frost and the curls on Nadenka's temples and the down on her upper lip were covered with silvery frost. She was holding my arm and we were standing on a high hill. From where we stood to the ground below there stretched a smooth sloping descent in which the sun was reflected as in a looking-glass. Beside us was a little sledge lined with bright red cloth.

"Let us go down, Nadyezhda Petrovna!" I besought her. "Only once! I assure you we shall be all right and not hurt."

But Nadenka was afraid. The slope from her little goloshes to the bottom of the ice hill seemed to her a terrible, immensely deep abyss. Her spirit failed her, and she held her breath as she looked down, when I merely suggested her getting into the sledge, but what would it be if she were to risk flying into the abyss! She would die, she would go out of her mind.

"I entreat you!" I said. "You mustn't be afraid! You know it's poor-spirited, it's cowardly!"

Nadenka gave way at last, and from her face I saw that she gave way in mortal dread. I sat her in the sledge, pale and trembling, put my arm round her and with her cast myself down the precipice.

The sledge flew like a bullet. The air cleft by our flight beat in our faces, roared, whistled in our ears, tore at us, nipped us cruelly in its anger, tried to tear our heads off our shoulders. We had hardly strength to breathe from the pressure of the wind. It seemed as though the devil himself had caught us in his claws and was dragging us with a roar to hell. Surrounding objects melted into one long furiously racing streak. . . another moment and it seemed we should perish.

"I love you, Nadya!" I said in a low voice.

The sledge began moving more and more slowly, the roar of the wind and the whirr of the runners was no longer so terrible, it was easier to breathe, and at last we were at the bottom. Nadenka was more dead than alive. She was pale and scarcely breathing. . . I helped her to get up.

"Nothing would induce me to go again," she said, looking at me with wide eyes full of horror. "Nothing in the world! I almost died!"

A little later she recovered herself and looked enquiringly into my eyes, wondering had I really uttered those four words or had she fancied them in the roar of the hurricane. And I stood beside her smoking and looking attentively at my glove.

She took my arm and we spent a long while walking near the ice-hill. The riddle evidently would not let her rest. . . Had those words been uttered or not? . . . Yes or no? Yes or no? It was the question of pride, or honour, of life—a very important question, the most important question in the world. Nadenka kept impatiently, sorrowfully looking into my face with a penetrating glance; she answered at random, waiting to see whether I would not speak. Oh, the play of feeling on that sweet face! I saw that she was struggling with herself, that she wanted to say something, to ask some question, but she could not find the words; she felt awkward and frightened and troubled by her joy. . .

"Do you know what," she said without looking at me.

"Well?" I asked.

"Let us. . . slide down again."

We clambered up the ice-hill by the steps again. I sat Nadenka, pale and trembling, in the sledge; again we flew into the terrible abyss, again the wind roared and the runners whirred, and again when the flight of our sledge was at its swiftest and noisiest, I said in a low voice:

"I love you, Nadenka!"

When the sledge stopped, Nadenka flung a glance at the hill down which we had both slid, then bent a long look upon my face, listened to my voice which was unconcerned and passionless, and the whole of her little figure, every bit of it, even her muff and her hood expressed the utmost bewilderment, and on her face was written: "What does it mean? Who uttered *those* words? Did he, or did I only fancy it?"

The uncertainty worried her and drove her out of all patience. The poor girl did not answer my questions, frowned, and was on the point of tears.

"Hadn't we better go home?" I asked.

"Well, I. . . I like this tobogganning," she said, flushing. "Shall we go down once more?"

She "liked" the tobogganning, and yet as she got into the sledge she was, as both times before, pale, trembling, hardly able to breathe for terror.

We went down for the third time, and I saw she was looking at my face and watching my lips. But I put my handkerchief to my lips, coughed, and when we reached the middle of the hill I succeeded in bringing out:

"I love you, Nadya!"

And the mystery remained a mystery! Nadenka was silent, pondering on something. . . I saw her home, she tried to walk slowly, slackened her pace and kept waiting to see whether I would not say those words to her, and I saw how her soul was suffering, what effort she was making not to say to herself:

"It cannot be that the wind said them! And I don't want it to be the wind that said them!"

Next morning I got a little note:

"If you are tobogganing to-day, come for me.—N."

And from that time I began going every day tobogganing with Nadenka, and as we flew down in the sledge, every time I pronounced in a low voice the same words: "I love you, Nadya!"

Soon Nadenka grew used to that phrase as to alcohol or morphia. She could not live without it. It is true that flying down the ice-hill terrified her as before, but now the terror and danger gave a peculiar fascination to words of love—words which as before were a mystery and tantalized the soul. The same two—the wind and I were still suspected. . . Which of the two was making love to her she did not know, but apparently by now she did not care; from which goblet one drinks matters little if only the beverage is intoxicating.

It happened I went to the skating-ground alone at midday; mingling with the crowd I saw Nadenka go up to the ice-hill and look about for me. . . then she timidly mounted the steps. . . She was frightened of going alone—oh, how frightened! She was white as the snow, she was trembling, she went as though to the scaffold, but she went, she went without looking back, resolutely. She had evidently determined to put it to the test at last: would those sweet amazing words be heard when I was not there? I saw her, pale, her lips parted with horror, get into the sledge, shut her eyes and saying good-bye for ever to the earth, set off. . . "Whrrr!" whirred the runners. Whether Nadenka heard those words I do not know. I only saw her getting up from the sledge looking faint and exhausted. And one could tell from her face that she could not tell herself whether she had heard anything or not. Her terror while she had been flying down had deprived of her all power of hearing, of discriminating sounds, of understanding.

But then the month of March arrived. . . the spring sunshine was more kindly. . . Our ice-hill turned dark, lost its brilliance and finally melted. We gave up tobogganning. There was nowhere now where poor

Nadenka could hear those words, and indeed no one to utter them, since there was no wind and I was going to Petersburg—for long, perhaps for ever.

It happened two days before my departure I was sitting in the dusk in the little garden which was separated from the yard of Nadenka's house by a high fence with nails in it. . . It was still pretty cold, there was still snow by the manure heap, the trees looked dead but there was already the scent of spring and the rooks were cawing loudly as they settled for their night's rest. I went up to the fence and stood for a long while peeping through a chink. I saw Nadenka come out into the porch and fix a mournful yearning gaze on the sky. . . The spring wind was blowing straight into her pale dejected face. . . It reminded her of the wind which roared at us on the ice-hill when she heard those four words, and her face became very, very sorrowful, a tear trickled down her cheek, and the poor child held out both arms as though begging the wind to bring her those words once more. And waiting for the wind I said in a low voice:

"I love you, Nadya!"

Mercy! The change that came over Nadenka! She uttered a cry, smiled all over her face and looking joyful, happy and beautiful, held out her arms to meet the wind.

And I went off to pack up. . .

That was long ago. Now Nadenka is married; she married—whether of her own choice or not does not matter—a secretary of the Nobility Wardenship and now she has three children. That we once went tobogganning together, and that the wind brought her the words "I love you, Nadenka," is not forgotten; it is for her now the happiest, most touching, and beautiful memory in her life. . .

But now that I am older I cannot understand why I uttered those words, what was my motive in that joke. . .

A Country Cottage

Two young people who had not long been married were walking up and down the platform of a little country station. His arm was round her waist, her head was almost on his shoulder, and both were happy.

The moon peeped up from the drifting cloudlets and frowned, as it seemed, envying their happiness and regretting her tedious and utterly superfluous virginity. The still air was heavy with the fragrance of lilac and wild cherry. Somewhere in the distance beyond the line a corncrake was calling.

"How beautiful it is, Sasha, how beautiful!" murmured the young wife. "It all seems like a dream. See, how sweet and inviting that little copse looks! How nice those solid, silent telegraph posts are! They add a special note to the landscape, suggesting humanity, civilization in the distance. . . Don't you think it's lovely when the wind brings the rushing sound of a train?"

"Yes. . . But what hot little hands you've got. . . That's because you're excited, Varya. . . What have you got for our supper to-night?"

"Chicken and salad. . . It's a chicken just big enough for two. . . Then there is the salmon and sardines that were sent from town."

The moon as though she had taken a pinch of snuff hid her face behind a cloud. Human happiness reminded her of her own loneliness, of her solitary couch beyond the hills and dales.

"The train is coming!" said Varya, "how jolly!"

Three eyes of fire could be seen in the distance. The stationmaster came out on the platform. Signal lights flashed here and there on the line.

"Let's see the train in and go home," said Sasha, yawning. "What a splendid time we are having together, Varya, it's so splendid, one can hardly believe it's true!"

The dark monster crept noiselessly alongside the platform and came to a standstill. They caught glimpses of sleepy faces, of hats and shoulders at the dimly lighted windows.

"Look! look!" they heard from one of the carriages. "Varya and Sasha have come to meet us! There they are! . . . Varya! . . . Varya. . . Look!"

Two little girls skipped out of the train and hung on Varya's neck. They were followed by a stout, middle-aged lady, and a tall, lanky gentleman with grey whiskers; behind them came two schoolboys, laden with bags, and after the schoolboys, the governess, after the governess the grandmother.

"Here we are, here we are, dear boy!" began the whiskered gentleman, squeezing Sasha's hand. "Sick of waiting for us, I expect! You have been pitching into your old uncle for not coming down all this time, I daresay! Kolya, Kostya, Nina, Fifa. . . children! Kiss your cousin Sasha! We're all here, the whole troop of us, just for three or four days. . . I hope we shan't be too many for you? You mustn't let us put you out!"

At the sight of their uncle and his family, the young couple were horror-stricken. While his uncle talked and kissed them, Sasha had a vision of their little cottage: he and Varya giving up their three little rooms, all the pillows and bedding to their guests; the salmon, the sardines, the chicken all devoured in a single instant; the cousins plucking the flowers in their little garden, spilling the ink, filled the cottage with noise and confusion; his aunt talking continually about her ailments and her papa's having been Baron von Fintich. . .

And Sasha looked almost with hatred at his young wife, and whispered:

"It's you they've come to see! . . . Damn them!"

"No, it's you," answered Varya, pale with anger. "They're your relations! they're not mine!"

And turning to her visitors, she said with a smile of welcome: "Welcome to the cottage!"

The moon came out again. She seemed to smile, as though she were glad she had no relations. Sasha, turning his head away to hide his angry despairing face, struggled to give a note of cordial welcome to his voice as he said:

"It is jolly of you! Welcome to the cottage!"

A Blunder

Ilya Sergeitch Peplov and his wife Kleopatra Petrovna were standing at the door, listening greedily. On the other side in the little drawing-room a love scene was apparently taking place between two persons: their daughter Natashenka and a teacher of the district school, called Shchupkin.

"He's rising!" whispered Peplov, quivering with impatience and rubbing his hands. "Now, Kleopatra, mind; as soon as they begin talking of their feelings, take down the ikon from the wall and we'll go in and bless them. . . We'll catch him. . . A blessing with an ikon is sacred and binding. . . He couldn't get out of it, if he brought it into court."

On the other side of the door this was the conversation:

"Don't go on like that!" said Shchupkin, striking a match against his checked trousers. "I never wrote you any letters!"

"I like that! As though I didn't know your writing!" giggled the girl with an affected shriek, continually peeping at herself in the glass. "I knew it at once! And what a queer man you are! You are a writing master, and you write like a spider! How can you teach writing if you write so badly yourself?"

"H'm! . . . That means nothing. The great thing in writing lessons is not the hand one writes, but keeping the boys in order. You hit one on the head with a ruler, make another kneel down. . . Besides, there's nothing in handwriting! Nekrassov was an author, but his handwriting's a disgrace, there's a specimen of it in his collected works."

"You are not Nekrassov. . ." (A sigh). "I should love to marry an author. He'd always be writing poems to me."

"I can write you a poem, too, if you like."

"What can you write about?"

"Love—passion—your eyes. You'll be crazy when you read it. It would draw a tear from a stone! And if I write you a real poem, will you let me kiss your hand?"

"That's nothing much! You can kiss it now if you like."

Shchupkin jumped up, and making sheepish eyes, bent over the fat little hand that smelt of egg soap.

"Take down the ikon," Peplov whispered in a fluster, pale with excitement, and buttoning his coat as he prodded his wife with his elbow. "Come along, now!"

And without a second's delay Peplov flung open the door.

"Children," he muttered, lifting up his arms and blinking tearfully, "the Lord bless you, my children. May you live—be fruitful—and multiply."

"And—and I bless you, too," the mamma brought out, crying with happiness. "May you be happy, my dear ones! Oh, you are taking from me my only treasure!" she said to Shchupkin. "Love my girl, be good to her. . ."

Shchupkin's mouth fell open with amazement and alarm. The parents' attack was so bold and unexpected that he could not utter a single word.

"I'm in for it! I'm spliced!" he thought, going limp with horror. "It's all over with you now, my boy! There's no escape!"

And he bowed his head submissively, as though to say, "Take me, I'm vanquished."

"Ble-blessings on you," the papa went on, and he, too, shed tears. "Natashenka, my daughter, stand by his side. Kleopatra, give me the ikon."

But at this point the father suddenly left off weeping, and his face was contorted with anger.

"You ninny!" he said angrily to his wife. "You are an idiot! Is that the ikon?"

"Ach, saints alive!"

What had happened? The writing master raised himself and saw that he was saved; in her flutter the mamma had snatched from the wall the portrait of Lazhetchnikov, the author, in mistake for the ikon. Old Peplov and his wife stood disconcerted in the middle of the room, holding the portrait aloft, not knowing what to do or what to say. The writing master took advantage of the general confusion and slipped away.

Fat and Thin

Two friends—one a fat man and the other a thin man—met at the Nikolaevsky station. The fat man had just dined in the station and his greasy lips shone like ripe cherries. He smelt of sherry and *fleur d'orange*. The thin man had just slipped out of the train and was laden with portmanteaus, bundles, and bandboxes. He smelt of ham and coffee grounds. A thin woman with a long chin, his wife, and a tall schoolboy with one eye screwed up came into view behind his back.

"Porfiry," cried the fat man on seeing the thin man. "Is it you? My dear fellow! How many summers, how many winters!"

"Holy saints!" cried the thin man in amazement. "Misha! The friend of my childhood! Where have you dropped from?"

The friends kissed each other three times, and gazed at each other with eyes full of tears. Both were agreeably astounded.

"My dear boy!" began the thin man after the kissing. "This is unexpected! This is a surprise! Come have a good look at me! Just as handsome as I used to be! Just as great a darling and a dandy! Good gracious me! Well, and how are you? Made your fortune? Married? I am married as you see. . . This is my wife Luise, her maiden name was Vantsenbach. . . of the Lutheran persuasion. . . And this is my son Nafanail, a schoolboy in the third class. This is the friend of my childhood, Nafanya. We were boys at school together!"

Nafanail thought a little and took off his cap.

"We were boys at school together," the thin man went on. "Do you remember how they used to tease you? You were nicknamed Herostratus because you burned a hole in a schoolbook with a cigarette, and I was nicknamed Ephialtes because I was fond of telling tales. Ho—ho! . . . we were children! . . . Don't be shy, Nafanya. Go nearer to him. And this is my wife, her maiden name was Vantsenbach, of the Lutheran persuasion. . ."

Nafanail thought a little and took refuge behind his father's back.

"Well, how are you doing my friend?" the fat man asked, looking enthusiastically at his friend. "Are you in the service? What grade have you reached?"

"I am, dear boy! I have been a collegiate assessor for the last two years and I have the Stanislav. The salary is poor, but that's no great matter! The wife gives music lessons, and I go in for carving wooden cigarette cases in a private way. Capital cigarette cases! I sell them for a rouble each. If any one takes ten or more I make a reduction of course. We get along somehow. I served as a clerk, you know, and now I have been transferred here as a head clerk in the same department. I am going to serve here. And what about you? I bet you are a civil councillor by now? Eh?"

"No dear boy, go higher than that," said the fat man. "I have risen to privy councillor already. . . I have two stars."

The thin man turned pale and rigid all at once, but soon his face twisted in all directions in the broadest smile; it seemed as though sparks were flashing from his face and eyes. He squirmed, he doubled together, crumpled up. . . His portmanteaus, bundles and cardboard boxes seemed to shrink and crumple up too. . . His wife's long chin grew longer still; Nafanail drew himself up to attention and fastened all the buttons of his uniform.

"Your Excellency, I. . . delighted! The friend, one may say, of childhood and to have turned into such a great man! He—he!"

"Come, come!" the fat man frowned. "What's this tone for? You and I were friends as boys, and there is no need of this official obsequiousness!"

"Merciful heavens, your Excellency! What are you saying. . . ?" sniggered the thin man, wriggling more than ever. "Your Excellency's gracious attention is like refreshing manna. . . This, your Excellency, is my son Nafanail, . . . my wife Luise, a Lutheran in a certain sense."

The fat man was about to make some protest, but the face of the thin man wore an expression of such reverence, sugariness, and mawkish respectfulness that the privy councillor was sickened. He turned away from the thin man, giving him his hand at parting.

The thin man pressed three fingers, bowed his whole body and sniggered like a Chinaman: "He—he—he!" His wife smiled. Nafanail scraped with his foot and dropped his cap. All three were agreeably overwhelmed.

The Death of a Government Clerk

One fine evening, a no less fine government clerk called Ivan Dmitritch Tchervyakov was sitting in the second row of the stalls, gazing through an opera glass at the *Cloches de Corneville*. He gazed and felt at the acme of bliss. But suddenly. . . In stories one so often meets with this "But suddenly." The authors are right: life is so full of surprises! But suddenly his face puckered up, his eyes disappeared, his breathing was arrested. . . he took the opera glass from his eyes, bent over and. . . "Aptchee!!" he sneezed as you perceive. It is not reprehensible for anyone to sneeze anywhere. Peasants sneeze and so do police superintendents, and sometimes even privy councillors. All men sneeze. Tchervyakov was not in the least confused, he wiped his face with his handkerchief, and like a polite man, looked round to see whether he had disturbed any one by his sneezing. But then he was overcome with confusion. He saw that an old gentleman sitting in front of him in the first row of the stalls was carefully wiping his bald head and his neck with his glove and muttering something to himself. In the old gentleman, Tchervyakov recognised Brizzhalov, a civilian general serving in the Department of Transport.

"I have spattered him," thought Tchervyakov, "he is not the head of my department, but still it is awkward. I must apologise."

Tchervyakov gave a cough, bent his whole person forward, and whispered in the general's ear.

"Pardon, your Excellency, I spattered you accidentally. . ."

"Never mind, never mind."

"For goodness sake excuse me, I. . . I did not mean to."

"Oh, please, sit down! let me listen!"

Tchervyakov was embarrassed, he smiled stupidly and fell to gazing at the stage. He gazed at it but was no longer feeling bliss. He began to be troubled by uneasiness. In the interval, he went up to Brizzhalov, walked beside him, and overcoming his shyness, muttered:

"I spattered you, your Excellency, forgive me. . . you see. . . I didn't do it to. . ."

"Oh, that's enough. . . I'd forgotten it, and you keep on about it!" said the general, moving his lower lip impatiently.

"He has forgotten, but there is a fiendish light in his eye," thought Tchervyakov, looking suspiciously at the general. "And he doesn't want to talk. I ought to explain to him. . . that I really didn't intend. . . that it is the law of nature or else he will think I meant to spit on him. He doesn't think so now, but he will think so later!"

On getting home, Tchervyakov told his wife of his breach of good manners. It struck him that his wife took too frivolous a view of the incident; she was a little frightened, but when she learned that Brizzhalov was in a different department, she was reassured.

"Still, you had better go and apologise," she said, "or he will think you don't know how to behave in public."

"That's just it! I did apologise, but he took it somehow queerly. . . he didn't say a word of sense. There wasn't time to talk properly."

Next day Tchervyakov put on a new uniform, had his hair cut and went to Brizzhalov's to explain; going into the general's reception room he saw there a number of petitioners and among them the general himself, who was beginning to interview them. After questioning several petitioners the general raised his eyes and looked at Tchervyakov.

"Yesterday at the *Arcadia*, if you recollect, your Excellency," the latter began, "I sneezed and. . . accidentally spattered. . . Exc. . ."

"What nonsense. . . It's beyond anything! What can I do for you," said the general addressing the next petitioner.

"He won't speak," thought Tchervyakov, turning pale; "that means that he is angry. . . No, it can't be left like this. . . I will explain to him."

When the general had finished his conversation with the last of the petitioners and was turning towards his inner apartments, Tchervyakov took a step towards him and muttered:

"Your Excellency! If I venture to trouble your Excellency, it is simply from a feeling I may say of regret! . . . It was not intentional if you will graciously believe me."

The general made a lachrymose face, and waved his hand.

"Why, you are simply making fun of me, sir," he said as he closed the door behind him.

"Where's the making fun in it?" thought Tchervyakov, "there is nothing of the sort! He is a general, but he can't understand. If that is how it is I am not going to apologise to that *fanfaron* any more! The devil take him. I'll write a letter to him, but I won't go. By Jove, I won't."

So thought Tchervyakov as he walked home; he did not write a letter to the general, he pondered and pondered and could not make up that letter. He had to go next day to explain in person.

"I ventured to disturb your Excellency yesterday," he muttered, when the general lifted enquiring eyes upon him, "not to make fun as you were pleased to say. I was apologising for having spattered you in sneezing. . . And I did not dream of making fun of you. Should I dare to make fun of you, if we should take to making fun, then there would be no respect for persons, there would be. . ."

"Be off!" yelled the general, turning suddenly purple, and shaking all over.

"What?" asked Tchervyakov, in a whisper turning numb with horror.

"Be off!" repeated the general, stamping.

Something seemed to give way in Tchervyakov's stomach. Seeing nothing and hearing nothing he reeled to the door, went out into the street, and went staggering along. . . Reaching home mechanically, without taking off his uniform, he lay down on the sofa and died.

A PINK STOCKING

A Dull, rainy day. The sky is completely covered with heavy clouds, and there is no prospect of the rain ceasing. Outside sleet, puddles, and drenched jackdaws. Indoors it is half dark, and so cold that one wants the stove heated.

Pavel Petrovitch Somov is pacing up and down his study, grumbling at the weather. The tears of rain on the windows and the darkness of the room make him depressed. He is insufferably bored and has nothing to do. . . The newspapers have not been brought yet; shooting is out of the question, and it is not nearly dinner-time. . .

Somov is not alone in his study. Madame Somov, a pretty little lady in a light blouse and pink stockings, is sitting at his writing table. She is eagerly scribbling a letter. Every time he passes her as he strides up and down, Ivan Petrovitch looks over her shoulder at what she is writing. He sees big sprawling letters, thin and narrow, with all sorts of tails and flourishes. There are numbers of blots, smears, and finger-marks. Madame Somov does not like ruled paper, and every line runs downhill with horrid wriggles as it reaches the margin. . .

"Lidotchka, who is it you are writing such a lot to?" Somov inquires, seeing that his wife is just beginning to scribble the sixth page.

"To sister Varya."

"Hm. . . it's a long letter! I'm so bored—let me read it!"

"Here, you may read it, but there's nothing interesting in it."

Somov takes the written pages and, still pacing up and down, begins reading. Lidotchka leans her elbows on the back of her chair and watches the expression of his face. . . After the first page his face lengthens and an expression of something almost like panic comes into it. . . At the third page Somov frowns and scratches the back of his head. At the fourth he pauses, looks with a scared face at his wife, and seems to ponder. After thinking a little, he takes up the letter again with a sigh. . . His face betrays perplexity and even alarm. . ."

"Well, this is beyond anything!" he mutters, as he finishes reading the letter and flings the sheets on the table, "It's positively incredible!"

"What's the matter?" asks Lidotchka, flustered.

"What's the matter! You've covered six pages, wasted a good two hours scribbling, and there's nothing in it at all! If there were one tiny idea! One reads on and on, and one's brain is as muddled as though one were deciphering the Chinese wriggles on tea chests! Ough!"

"Yes, that's true, Vanya, . . ." says Lidotchka, reddening. "I wrote it carelessly. . ."

"Queer sort of carelessness! In a careless letter there is some meaning and style—there is sense in it—while yours. . . excuse me, but I don't know what to call it! It's absolute twaddle! There are words and sentences, but not the slightest sense in them. Your whole letter is exactly like the conversation of two boys: 'We had pancakes to-day! And we had a soldier come to see us!' You say the same thing over and over again! You drag it out, repeat yourself. . . The wretched ideas dance about like devils: there's no making out where anything begins, where anything ends. . . How can you write like that?"

"If I had been writing carefully," Lidotchka says in self defence, "then there would not have been mistakes. . ."

"Oh, I'm not talking about mistakes! The awful grammatical howlers! There's not a line that's not a personal insult to grammar! No stops nor commas—and the spelling. . . brrr! 'Earth' has an *a* in it!! And the writing! It's desperate! I'm not joking, Lida. . . I'm surprised and appalled at your letter. . . You mustn't be angry, darling, but, really, I had no idea you were such a duffer at grammar. . . And yet you belong to a cultivated, well-educated circle: you are the wife of a University man, and the daughter of a general! Tell me, did you ever go to school?"

"What next! I finished at the Von Mebke's boarding school. . ."

Somov shrugs his shoulders and continues to pace up and down, sighing. Lidotchka, conscious of her ignorance and ashamed of it, sighs too and casts down her eyes. . . Ten minutes pass in silence.

"You know, Lidotchka, it really is awful!" says Somov, suddenly halting in front of her and looking into her face with horror. "You are a mother. . . do you understand? A mother! How can you teach your children if you know nothing yourself? You have a good brain, but what's the use of it if you have never mastered the very rudiments of knowledge? There—never mind about knowledge. . . the children will get that at school, but, you know, you are very shaky on the moral side too! You sometimes use such language that it makes my ears tingle!"

Somov shrugs his shoulders again, wraps himself in the folds of his dressing-gown and continues his pacing. . . He feels vexed and injured, and at the same time sorry for Lidotchka, who does not protest, but

ANTON CHEKHOV

merely blinks. . . Both feel oppressed and miserable. . . Absorbed in their woes, they do not notice how time is passing and the dinner hour is approaching.

Sitting down to dinner, Somov, who is fond of good eating and of eating in peace, drinks a large glass of vodka and begins talking about something else. Lidotchka listens and assents, but suddenly over the soup her eyes fill with tears and she begins whimpering.

"It's all mother's fault!" she says, wiping away her tears with her dinner napkin. "Everyone advised her to send me to the high school, and from the high school I should have been sure to go on to the University!"

"University. . . high school," mutters Somov. "That's running to extremes, my girl! What's the good of being a blue stocking! A blue stocking is the very deuce! Neither man nor woman, but just something midway: neither one thing nor another. . . I hate blue stockings! I would never have married a learned woman. . ."

"There's no making you out. . .", says Lidotchka. "You are angry because I am not learned, and at the same time you hate learned women; you are annoyed because I have no ideas in my letter, and yet you yourself are opposed to my studying. . ."

"You do catch me up at a word, my dear," yawns Somov, pouring out a second glass of vodka in his boredom.

Under the influence of vodka and a good dinner, Somov grows more good-humoured, lively, and soft. . . He watches his pretty wife making the salad with an anxious face and a rush of affection for her, of indulgence and forgiveness comes over him.

"It was stupid of me to depress her, poor girl. . . ," he thought. "Why did I say such a lot of dreadful things? She is silly, that's true, uncivilised and narrow; but. . . there are two sides to the question, and *audiatur et altera pars* . . . Perhaps people are perfectly right when they say that woman's shallowness rests on her very vocation. Granted that it is her vocation to love her husband, to bear children, and to mix salad, what the devil does she want with learning? No, indeed!"

At that point he remembers that learned women are usually tedious, that they are exacting, strict, and unyielding; and, on the other hand, how easy it is to get on with silly Lidotchka, who never pokes her nose into anything, does not understand so much, and never obtrudes her criticism. There is peace and comfort with Lidotchka, and no risk of being interfered with.

"Confound them, those clever and learned women! It's better and easier to live with simple ones," he thinks, as he takes a plate of chicken from Lidotchka.

He recollects that a civilised man sometimes feels a desire to talk and share his thoughts with a clever and well-educated woman. "What of it?" thinks Somov. "If I want to talk of intellectual subjects, I'll go to Natalya Andreyevna. . . or to Marya Frantsovna. . . It's very simple! But no, I shan't go. One can discuss intellectual subjects with men," he finally decides.

At a Summer Villa

I Love You. You are my life, my happiness—everything to me! Forgive the avowal, but I have not the strength to suffer and be silent. I ask not for love in return, but for sympathy. Be at the old arbour at eight o'clock this evening. . . To sign my name is unnecessary I think, but do not be uneasy at my being anonymous. I am young, nice-looking. . . what more do you want?"

When Pavel Ivanitch Vyhodtsev, a practical married man who was spending his holidays at a summer villa, read this letter, he shrugged his shoulders and scratched his forehead in perplexity.

"What devilry is this?" he thought. "I'm a married man, and to send me such a queer. . . silly letter! Who wrote it?"

Pavel Ivanitch turned the letter over and over before his eyes, read it through again, and spat with disgust.

"'I love you'" . . . he said jeeringly. "A nice boy she has pitched on! So I'm to run off to meet you in the arbour! . . . I got over all such romances and *fleurs d'amour* years ago, my girl. . . Hm! She must be some reckless, immoral creature. . . Well, these women are a set! What a whirligig—God forgive us!—she must be to write a letter like that to a stranger, and a married man, too! It's real demoralisation!"

In the course of his eight years of married life Pavel Ivanitch had completely got over all sentimental feeling, and he had received no letters from ladies except letters of congratulation, and so, although he tried to carry it off with disdain, the letter quoted above greatly intrigued and agitated him.

An hour after receiving it, he was lying on his sofa, thinking:

"Of course I am not a silly boy, and I am not going to rush off to this idiotic rendezvous; but yet it would be interesting to know who wrote it! Hm. . . It is certainly a woman's writing. . . The letter is written with genuine feeling, and so it can hardly be a joke. . . Most likely it's some neurotic girl, or perhaps a widow. . . widows are frivolous and eccentric as a rule. Hm. . . Who could it be?"

What made it the more difficult to decide the question was that Pavel Ivanitch had not one feminine acquaintance among all the summer visitors, except his wife.

"It is queer. . ." he mused. "'I love you!' . . . When did she manage to fall in love? Amazing woman! To fall in love like this, apropos of nothing, without making any acquaintance and finding out what sort of man I am. . . She must be extremely young and romantic if she is capable of falling in love after two or three looks at me. . . But. . . who is she?"

Pavel Ivanitch suddenly recalled that when he had been walking among the summer villas the day before, and the day before that, he had several times been met by a fair young lady with a light blue hat and a turn-up nose. The fair charmer had kept looking at him, and when he sat down on a seat she had sat down beside him. . .

"Can it be she?" Vyhodtsev wondered. "It can't be! Could a delicate ephemeral creature like that fall in love with a worn-out old eel like me? No, it's impossible!"

At dinner Pavel Ivanitch looked blankly at his wife while he meditated:

"She writes that she is young and nice-looking. . . So she's not old. . . Hm. . . To tell the truth, honestly I am not so old and plain that no one could fall in love with me. My wife loves me! Besides, love is blind, we all know. . ."

"What are you thinking about?" his wife asked him.

"Oh. . . my head aches a little. . ." Pavel Ivanitch said, quite untruly.

He made up his mind that it was stupid to pay attention to such a nonsensical thing as a love-letter, and laughed at it and at its authoress, but—alas!—powerful is the "dacha" enemy of mankind! After dinner, Pavel Ivanitch lay down on his bed, and instead of going to sleep, reflected:

"But there, I daresay she is expecting me to come! What a silly! I can just imagine what a nervous fidget she'll be in and how her *tournure* will quiver when she does not find me in the arbour! I shan't go, though. . . Bother her!"

But, I repeat, powerful is the enemy of mankind.

"Though I might, perhaps, just out of curiosity. . ." he was musing, half an hour later. "I might go and look from a distance what sort of a creature she is. . . It would be interesting to have a look at her! It would be fun, and that's all! After all, why shouldn't I have a little fun since such a chance has turned up?"

Pavel Ivanitch got up from his bed and began dressing. "What are you getting yourself up so smartly for?" his wife asked, noticing that he was putting on a clean shirt and a fashionable tie.

"Oh, nothing. . . I must have a walk. . . My head aches. . . Hm."

Pavel Ivanitch dressed in his best, and waiting till eight o'clock, went out of the house. When the figures of gaily dressed summer visitors of both sexes began passing before his eyes against the bright green background, his heart throbbed.

"Which of them is it? . . ." he wondered, advancing irresolutely. "Come, what am I afraid of? Why, I am not going to the rendezvous! What. . . a fool! Go forward boldly! And what if I go into the arbour? Well, well. . . there is no reason I should."

Pavel Ivanitch's heart beat still more violently. . . Involuntarily, with no desire to do so, he suddenly pictured to himself the half-darkness of the arbour. . . A graceful fair girl with a little blue hat and a turn-up nose rose before his imagination. He saw her, abashed by her love and trembling all over, timidly approach him, breathing excitedly, and. . . suddenly clasping him in her arms.

"If I weren't married it would be all right. . ." he mused, driving sinful ideas out of his head. "Though. . . for once in my life, it would do no harm to have the experience, or else one will die without knowing what. . . And my wife, what will it matter to her? Thank God, for eight years I've never moved one step away from her. . . Eight years of irreproachable duty! Enough of her. . . It's positively vexatious. . . I'm ready to go to spite her!"

Trembling all over and holding his breath, Pavel Ivanitch went up to the arbour, wreathed with ivy and wild vine, and peeped into it. . . A smell of dampness and mildew reached him. . .

"I believe there's nobody. . ." he thought, going into the arbour, and at once saw a human silhouette in the corner.

The silhouette was that of a man. . . Looking more closely, Pavel Ivanitch recognised his wife's brother, Mitya, a student, who was staying with them at the villa.

"Oh, it's you. . ." he growled discontentedly, as he took off his hat and sat down.

"Yes, it's I" . . . answered Mitya.

Two minutes passed in silence.

"Excuse me, Pavel Ivanitch," began Mitya: "but might I ask you to leave me alone?? . . . I am thinking over the dissertation for my degree and. . . and the presence of anybody else prevents my thinking."

"You had better go somewhere in a dark avenue. . ." Pavel Ivanitch observed mildly. "It's easier to think in the open air, and, besides, . . . er. . . I should like to have a little sleep here on this seat. . . It's not so hot here. . ."

"You want to sleep, but it's a question of my dissertation. . ." Mitya grumbled. "The dissertation is more important."

Again there was a silence. Pavel Ivanitch, who had given the rein to his imagination and was continually hearing footsteps, suddenly leaped up and said in a plaintive voice:

"Come, I beg you, Mitya! You are younger and ought to consider me. . . I am unwell and. . . I need sleep. . . Go away!"

"That's egoism. . . Why must you be here and not I? I won't go as a matter of principle."

"Come, I ask you to! Suppose I am an egoist, a despot and a fool. . . but I ask you to go! For once in my life I ask you a favour! Show some consideration!"

Mitya shook his head.

"What a beast!. . ." thought Pavel Ivanitch. "That can't be a rendezvous with him here! It's impossible with him here!"

"I say, Mitya," he said, "I ask you for the last time. . . Show that you are a sensible, humane, and cultivated man!"

"I don't know why you keep on so!" . . . said Mitya, shrugging his shoulders. "I've said I won't go, and I won't. I shall stay here as a matter of principle. . ."

At that moment a woman's face with a turn-up nose peeped into the arbour. . .

Seeing Mitya and Pavel Ivanitch, it frowned and vanished.

"She is gone!" thought Pavel Ivanitch, looking angrily at Mitya. "She saw that blackguard and fled! It's all spoilt!"

After waiting a little longer, he got up, put on his hat and said:

"You're a beast, a low brute and a blackguard! Yes! A beast! It's mean. . . and silly! Everything is at an end between us!"

"Delighted to hear it!" muttered Mitya, also getting up and putting on his hat. "Let me tell you that by being here just now you've played me such a dirty trick that I'll never forgive you as long as I live."

Pavel Ivanitch went out of the arbour, and beside himself with rage, strode rapidly to his villa. Even the sight of the table laid for supper did not soothe him.

"Once in a lifetime such a chance has turned up," he thought in agitation; "and then it's been prevented! Now she is offended. . . crushed!"

At supper Pavel Ivanitch and Mitya kept their eyes on their plates and maintained a sullen silence. . . They were hating each other from the bottom of their hearts.

"What are you smiling at?" asked Pavel Ivanitch, pouncing on his wife. "It's only silly fools who laugh for nothing!"

His wife looked at her husband's angry face, and went off into a peal of laughter.

"What was that letter you got this morning?" she asked.

"I? . . . I didn't get one. . ." Pavel Ivanitch was overcome with confusion. "You are inventing. . . imagination."

"Oh, come, tell us! Own up, you did! Why, it was I sent you that letter! Honour bright, I did! Ha ha!"

Pavel Ivanitch turned crimson and bent over his plate. "Silly jokes," he growled.

"But what could I do? Tell me that. . . We had to scrub the rooms out this evening, and how could we get you out of the house? There was no other way of getting you out. . . But don't be angry, stupid. . . I didn't want you to be dull in the arbour, so I sent the same letter to Mitya too! Mitya, have you been to the arbour?"

Mitya grinned and left off glaring with hatred at his rival.

A Note About the Author

Anton Chekhov (1860–1904) was a Russian doctor, short-story writer, and playwright. Born in the port city of Taganrog, Chekhov was the third child of Pavel, a grocer and devout Christian, and Yevgeniya, a natural storyteller. His father, a violent and arrogant man, abused his wife and children and would serve as the inspiration for many of the writer's most tyrannical and hypocritical characters. Chekhov studied at the Greek School in Taganrog, where he learned Ancient Greek. In 1876, his father's debts forced the family to relocate to Moscow, where they lived in poverty while Anton remained in Taganrog to settle their finances and finish his studies. During this time, he worked odd jobs while reading extensively and composing his first written works. He joined his family in Moscow in 1879, pursuing a medical degree while writing short stories for entertainment and to support his parents and siblings. In 1876, after finishing his degree and contracting tuberculosis, he began writing for St. Petersburg's *Novoye Vremya*, a popular paper which helped him to launch his literary career and gain financial independence. A friend and colleague of Leo Tolstoy, Maxim Gorky, and Ivan Bunin, Chekhov is remembered today for his skillful observations of everyday Russian life, his deeply psychological character studies, and his mastery of language and the rhythms of conversation.

A Note from the Publisher

Spanning many genres, from non-fiction essays to literature classics to children's books and lyric poetry, Mint Edition books showcase the master works of our time in a modern new package. The text is freshly typeset, is clean and easy to read, and features a new note about the author in each volume. Many books also include exclusive new introductory material. Every book boasts a striking new cover, which makes it as appropriate for collecting as it is for gift giving. Mint Edition books are only printed when a reader orders them, so natural resources are not wasted. We're proud that our books are never manufactured in excess and exist only in the exact quantity they need to be read and enjoyed.

bookfinity™

Discover more of your favorite classics with Bookfinity™.

- Track your reading with custom book lists.
- Get great book recommendations for your personalized Reader Type.
- Add reviews for your favorite books.
- AND MUCH MORE!

Visit **bookfinity.com** and take the fun Reader Type quiz to get started.

Enjoy our classic and modern companion pairings!

Printed in the USA
CPSIA information can be obtained
at www.ICGtesting.com
JSHW021416160824
R13664500001B/R136645PG68134JSX00017B/83

9 781513 264776